The Beach
of Dreams

The Beach of Dreams

Henry De Vere Stacpoole

MINT EDITIONS

The Beach of Dreams was first published in 1919.

This edition published by Mint Editions 2021.

ISBN 9781513283814 | E-ISBN 9781513288833

Published by Mint Editions®

 MINT
EDITIONS

minteditionbooks.com

Publishing Director: Jennifer Newens
Design & Production: Rachel Lopez Metzger
Project Manager: Micaela Clark
Typesetting: Westchester Publishing Services

Contents

PART I

I

The Albatross

The fo'c'sle, lit by a teapot lamp, shewed the port watch in their bunks, snoring, all but Harbutt and Raft seated on a chest, Harbutt patching a pair of trousers, Raft smoking.

Raft was a big red-headed man with eyes that seemed always roving over great distances as though in search of something. He was thirty-two years of age and he had used the sea since twelve—twenty years. His past was a long succession of fo'c'sles, bar-rooms, blazing suns, storms and sea happenings so run together that all sequence was lost. Beyond them lay a dismal blotch, his childhood. He had entered the world and literally and figuratively had been laid at the door of a workhouse; of his childhood he remembered little, of his parentage he knew nothing. In drink he was quiet, but most dangerous under certain provocations.

It was as though deep in his being lay a blazing hatred born of injustice through ages and only coming to light when upborne by balloon-juice. On these occasions a saloon bar with its glitter and phantom show of mirth and prosperity sometimes called on him to dispense and destroy it, the passion to fight the crowd seized him, a passion that has its origin, perhaps, in sources other than alcohol.

He was talking now to Harbutt, scarcely lowering his voice on account of the fellows in the bunks. Snoring and drugged with ozone a kick would only have made them curse and turn on the other side, and as he talked his voice made part of that procession of noises inseparable from the fo'c'sle of a ship under sail against a head sea. He had been holding forth on the food and general conditions of this ship compared with the food and conditions of his last, when Harbutt cut in.

"There's not a pin to choose between owners, and ships is owners as far as a sailorman's concerned.—Blast them."

"I was in a hooker once," said Raft, "and the Old Man came across a lot of cheap sugar, served it out to save the m'lasses. It was lead, most of it, and the chaps that swallowed it their teeth came out."

"What happened to them then?"

"They croaked. I joined at Bombay, after the business, or I'd have croaked too."

"What ship was that?" asked Harbutt.

"I've forgot her name, it was a good bit back—but it's the truth."

"Of course it's the truth," replied the other, "who's doubtin' you, any dog's trick played on a sailorman's the truth, you can lay to that. I've had four years of sea and I oughta know."

"What's this you were?" asked Raft.

"Oh, I was a lot o' things," replied Harbutt. "Wished I'd never left them to join this b—y business, but it's the same ashore, owners all the time stuffin' themselves and gettin' rich, workers starvin'."

Raft belonged to the old time labour world dating from Pelagon, he grumbled, but had no grudge against owners in general, it was only in drink that Pelagon rose in him. Harbutt was an atom of the new voice that is heard everywhere now, even in fo'c'sles. He had failed in everything on land and a'board ship he was a slacker. You cannot be a voice and an A.B. at the same time.

"What was your last job ashore?" went on Raft with the persistence of a child, always wanting to know.

"Cleanin' out pig sties," said Harbutt viciously. "Drove to it. I tell you when a chap's down he's down, the chaps that has money tramples on the chaps that hasn't. I've been through it and I know. It's the rich man does it."

"Well," said Raft, "I don't even remember seeing one."

"Haven't you ever been in no cities?"

"I've been in cities right enough, but most by the water-side."

"Well, you've seen chaps in plug hats and chaps drivin' in carriages, that's the sort that keeps us down, that's the sort we've got to make an end of."

Raft did not quite see. He had a respect for Harbutt mixed with a contempt for him as a sailor. Harbutt knew a lot—but he could not see how the chaps in plug hats kept other people down; the few he had seen had always seemed to him away and beyond his world, soft folk, and always busy about their own affairs—and how were they to be made an end of?

"Do you mean killing them?" he asked.

"Oh, there's other ways than killin'," replied Harbutt. "It's not them, it's their money does the trick."

He finished his patch and turned in. Raft finished his pipe and turned in also and the fo'c'sle was given over to the noises of the sea and the straining timbers of the ship.

Now that the figures of the two sailors had vanished its personality took fuller life, grim, dark, close, like the interior of a grimy hand clutching the lives of all those sleepers. The beams shewed like the curved fingers, and the heel of the bowsprit like the point of the in-turned thumb, a faint soul-killing rock of kerosene filled it, intensifying, after the fashion of ambergris, all the other perfumes, without losing in power. Bilge, tobacco and humanity, you cannot know what these things are till they are married with the reek of kerosene, with the grunts and snores of weary men, with lamplight dimmed with smoke haze; with the heave and fall of the sea; the groaning of timbers and the boom of the waves. This is the fo'c'sle whose great, great, great grandmother was the lower deck of the trireme where slaves chained to benches laboured till they died, just as they labour today.

II

North-West

The *Albatross*, bound from Cape Town to Melbourne, had been blown out of her course and south of the Crozet Islands; she was now steering north-west, making towards Kerguelen, across an ice-blue sea, vast, like a country of broken crystal strewn with snow. The sky, against which the top-gallant stay-sails shewed gull-white in the sun, had the cold blue of the sea and was hung round at the horizon by clouds like the white clouds that hang round the Pacific Trades.

Raft was at the wheel and Captain Pound the master was pacing the deck with Mason the first officer, up and down, pausing now and then for a glance away to windward, now with an eye aloft at the steadfast canvas, talking all the time of subjects half a world away.

It was a sociable ship as far as the afterguard was concerned. Pound being a rough and capable man of the old school with no false dignity and an open manner of speech. He had been talking of his little house at Twickenham, of Mrs. Pound and the children, of servants and neighbours that were unsociable and now he was talking of dreams. He had been dreaming the night before of Pembroke docks, the port he had started from as a boy. Pembroke docks was a bad dream for Pound, and he said so. It always heralded some disaster when it appeared before him in dreamland.

"I've always dreamt before that I was starting from there," said he, "but last night I was getting the old *Albatross* in, and the tow rope went, and the tug knocked herself to bits, and then the old hooker swung round and there was Mrs. P. on the quayside in her night attire shouting to me to put the helm down—under hare sticks in the docks, mind you!"

"Dreams are crazy things," said Mason. "I don't believe there's anything in them."

"Well, maybe not," said Pound. He glanced at the binnacle card and then went below.

Nothing is more impressive to the unaccustomed mind than the spars and canvas of a ship under full sail seen from the deck, nothing more suggestive of power and the daring of man than the sight of those leviathan spars and vast sail spaces rising dizzily from main and foresail in pyramids to where the truck works like a pencil point writing on the sky. Nothing more arresting than the power of the steersman. A turn of the wheel in the hands of Raft would set all that canvas shuddering or thundering, spilling the wind as the water is spilled from a reservoir, a moment's indecision or slackness might lose the ship a mile on her course. But Raft steered as he breathed, automatically, almost unconsciously, almost without effort. He, who ashore was hopelessly adrift and without guidance, at the helm was all wisdom, direction and intuition.

The wake of the *Albatross* lay as if drawn with a ruler.

His trick was nearly up, and when he was relieved he went forward; pausing at the fo'c'sle head to light a pipe he fell in talk with some of the hands, leaning with his back against the bulwarks and blown upon by the spill of the wind from the head sails.

An old shell-back by name of Ponting was holding the floor.

"We're comin' up to Kerguelen," he was saying. "Should think I did know it. Put in there in a sealer out of New Bedford in '82. I wasn't more'n a boy then. The Yanks used to use that place a lot in those days. The blackest blastedest hole I ever struck. Christmas Island was where we lay mostly, for two months, the chaps huntin' the wal'uses and killin' more than they could carry. The blastedest hole I ever struck."

"I was there in a Dane once," began another of the crew. "It was time of year the sea cows was matin' and you could hear the roarin' of them ten mile off."

"Dane," said Ponting, "what made you ship a'board a Dane—I've heard tell of Danes. Knew a chap signed on in one of them Leith boots out of Copenhagen runnin' north, one of them old North Sea cattle trucks turned into a passenger tramp, passengers and ponies with a hundred ton of hay stowed forward and the passengers lyin' on their backs on it smokin' their pipes, and the bridge crawled over with passengers, girls and children, and the chap at the wheel havin' to push 'em out of the way, kept hittin' reefs all the run from Leith to God knows where, and the Old Man playin' the fiddle most of the time."

"That chap said the Danes was a d——d lot too sociable for him."

Raft listened without entirely comprehending. He had always been a fore-mast hand. He knew practically nothing of steam and he would just as soon have fancied himself a railway porter as a hand on a passenger ship. He was one of the old school of merchant seamen and the idea of a cargo of girls and children and general passengers, not to speak of ponies, was beyond him.

The girls he had mostly known were of the wharf-side. He finished his pipe and went down below—and turned in.

He was rousted out by the voice of the Bo'sw'n calling for all hands on deck and slipping into his oilskins he came up, receiving a smack of sea in his face as he emerged from the fo'c'sle hatch. The wind had shifted and a black squall coming up from astern had hit the ship. More was coming and through the sheeting rain and spindrift the voice of the Bo'sw'n was roaring to let go the fore top-gallant halyards.

Next moment Raft was in the rigging followed by others. The sail had to be stowed. The wind tried to tear him loose and the sheeting rain to drown him, but he went on clinging to the top-gallant mast-stays and looking down he could see the faces of the others following him, faces sheeted over with rain and working blindly upwards.

Ponting was the man immediately below him, and taking breath for a moment and against the wind, Ponting was now yelling out that they had their work cut out for them.

They had.

The top-gallant sail had taken charge of itself, and Raft and Ponting as they lay out on the yard seemed battling with a thing alive, intelligent, and desperately wicked.

The sail snored and trembled and sang, standing out in great hoods and folds, hard as steel; now it would yield, owing to a slackening of the wind, and then, like a brute that had only been waiting to take them by surprise, it would burst out again, releasing itself, whilst the yard buckled and sprang, almost casting them from it.

Then began a battle fought without a sound or cry except the bubbling and snoring of the great sail struggling for its wicked liberty, it shrank and they flung themselves on it, it bellied and flung them back, clinging to the lift they saved themselves, attacking it again with the dumb fury of dogs or wolves on a fighting prey. Twenty times it tried to destroy them and twenty times they all but had it under.

The fight died out of the monster for a moment and Raft had nearly an armful of it in when it stiffened, fighting free of him, owing to Ponting and the other fellow not having made good. They clung for a moment without moving, resting, and Raft glancing down saw far away below the narrow deck driving wedge-like through the foam-capped seas.

Then the struggle began again. The sail, like its would-be captors,

HENRY DE VERE STACPOOLE

seemed also to have taken breath, it held firm, relaxed, banged out again in thunder, developed new hoods and folds as a struggling monster might develop new heads and kinks, and then, all of a sudden when it seemed that no effort was of avail the end came.

The wind paused for a moment, as if gathering up all its strength against the dogged persistency which is man, and in that moment the three on the yard had the sail under their chests beating and crushing the life out of it. Then the gaskets were passed round it and they clung for a moment to rest and breathe.

It was nothing, or they thought nothing of it, this battle for life with a monster, just the stowing of a top-gallant sail in dirty weather, and most likely when they got down the Bo'sw'n would call them farmers for being such a time over it. Meanwhile they clung idly for a moment, partly to rest and partly to look at something worth seeing.

The squall was blowing out, there was nothing behind it and away on the port quarter the almost setting sun had broken through the smother and was lighting the sea.

There, set in a thousand square acres of snowcapped tourmaline, white as a gull and beautiful as grace itself, was running a vessel under bare poles. The two yellow funnels, the cut of the hull, told Ponting what she was. He had seen her twice before and no sailor who had once set eyes on her could forget her.

"See that blighter," he yelled across to Raft. "Know her?"

"Should think I did, she's the *Gaston de Paree*—a yacht—seen her in T'lon."

Then they came down, crawling like weary men, and on deck no one abused them for their slackness or the time they'd been over their job. The *Albatross* was running easy and the Bo'sw'n with others was taken up with a momentary curiosity over the great white yacht.

No one knew her but Ponting, who had for several years acted as deck hand on some of the Mediterranean boats.

"I know her," said he ranging up beside the others. "She's the *Gaston de Paree*, a yot—seen her in T'lon harbour and seen her again at Suez, she's a thousand tonner, y'can't mistake them funnels nor the width of them, she's a twenty knotter and the chap that owns her is a king or somethin'; last time I saw her she was off to the China seas, they say she's all cluttered up with dredges and dipsy gear, and she mostly spends her time takin' soundin's and scrabblin' up shell fish and such— that's his way of amusin' himself."

"Then he must be crazy," said the Bo'sw'n, "but b'God he's got a beauty under him—what's he doin' down here away?"

"Ax me another," said Ponting. Raft stood with the others, watching the *Gaston de Paris* from whose funnels now the smoke was coming festooned on the wind, then he went below to shed his oilskins and smoke.

She had ceased to interest him.

III

THE GASTON DE PARIS

O ld Ponting was right in all his particulars, except one. The owner of the *Gaston de Paris* was not a king, only a prince.

Prince Selm, a gentleman like his Highness of Monaco with a passion for the deep sea and its exploration. The Holy Roman Empire had given his great grandfather the title of prince, and estates in Thuringia gave him money enough to do what he pleased, an unfortunate marriage gave him a distaste for High Civilization, and his scientific bent and passion for the sea—inherited with a strain of old Norse blood—did the rest.

He had chosen well. Cards, women and wine, pleasure and the glittering things of life, all these betray one, but the sea, though she may kill, never leaves a man broken, never destroys his soul.

But Eugene Henry William of Selm for all this sea passion might have remained a landsman, for the simple reason that he was one of those thorough souls for whom Life and an Object are synonymous terms. In other words he would never have made a yachtsman, a creature shifting from Keil to Cowes and Cowes to Naples according to season, a cup gatherer and club-house haunter.

But Exploration gave him the incentive and the Musée Océanographique of Monaco his inspiration, limitless wealth supplied the means.

The *Gaston de Paris* built by Viguard of Toulon was an ocean going steam yacht of twelve hundred and fifty tons with engines by Conturier of Nantes and everything of the latest from Conturier's twin-action centrifugal bilge pumps to the last thing in sea valves. She was reckoned by those who knew her the finest sea-going yacht in the world and she was certainly the *chef-d'oeuvre* of Lafiette, Viguard's chief designer. Lafiette was more than a designer, he was a creator, the sea was in his blood giving him that touch of genius or madness, that something eccentric which made him at times cast rules and formulae aside.

The decks of the *Gaston de Paris* ran flush, with little encumbrance save a deck-house forward given over to electrical and deep sea instruments.

Forward of the engine room and right to the bulkheads of the fo'c'sle ran a lower deck reached by a hatch aft of the instrument room. Here were stowed the dredges and buoys and all the gear belonging to them, trawl nets and deep sea traps, cable and spare rope and sounding-wire, harpoons and grancs and a hundred odds and ends, all in order and spick and span as the gear of a warship.

Aft of the engine-room the yacht was a little palace. Prince Selm would labour like any of his crew over a net coming in or in an emergency, but he ate off silver and slept between sheets of exceedingly fine linen. Though a sailor, almost one might say a fisherman, he was always Monsieur le Prince and though his hobby lay in the depths of the sea his intellect did not lie there too. Politics, Literature and Art travelled with him as mind companions, whilst in the flesh he often managed to bring off with him on his "outlandish expeditions" more or less pleasant people from the great world where Civilisation sits in cities, feeding Art and Philosophy, Science and Literature with the hearts and souls of men.

The main saloon of the *Gaston de Paris* fought in all its details against the idea of shipboard life, the gilt and scrolls of the yacht decorator, the mirrors, and all the rest of his abominations were not to be found here, panels by Chardin painted for Madame de Pompadour occupied the walls, the main lamp, a flying dragon by Benvenuto Cellini, clutching in its claws a globe of fire, had, for satellites, four torch bearers of bronze by Claus, a library, writing and smoking room, combined, opened from the main saloon, and there was a boudoir decorated in purple and pearl with flower pictures by Lactropius unfaded despite their date of 1685.

Nothing could be stranger to the mind than the contrast between the fo'c'sle of the *Albatross* and the after cabins of the *Gaston*, nothing, except, maybe, the contrast between a garret in Montmartre or Stepney and a drawing-room in the Avenue du Trocadéro or Mayfair.

Dinner was served on board the *Gaston de Paris* at seven, and tonight the Prince and his four guests, seated beneath the flying dragon of Cellini and enjoying their soup, held converse together light-heartedly and with a spirit that had been somewhat lacking of late. Every sea voyage has its periods of depression due to monotony; they had not sighted a ship for over ten days, and this evening the glimpse of the *Albatross* revealed through the break in the weather had in some curious way shattered the sense of isolation and broken the monotony. The four guests of the Prince were: Madame la Comtesse de Warens, an old lady with a passion for travel, a free thinker, whose mother was a friend of Voltaire in her youth and whose father had been a member of the Jacobin club; she was eighty-four years of age, declared herself indestructible by time, and her one last ambition to be a burial at sea. She was also a Socialistic-Anarchist, possessed an income of some forty thousand pounds a year derived from speculations of her late husband conducted during the war with Germany in 1870, yet was never known to give a sou to charity; her hands were all but the hands of a skeleton and covered with jewels, she smoked cigarettes incessantly. She was one of those old women whose energy seems to increase with age, tireless as a gnat she was always the last in bed and the first on deck, though lying in her bunk half the night reading French novels of which she had a trunkful and smoking her eternal cigarettes.

Beside her sat her niece, Cléo de Bromsart, English on the mother's side and educated in England, a girl of twenty, unmarried, dark-haired, fragile and beautiful as a dream. She was one of the old nobility, without dilution, yet strangely enough with money, for the Bromsarts, without marrying into trade, had adapted themselves to the new times so cleverly that Eugène de Bromsart the last of his race had retired from life leaving his only daughter and the last of her race wealthy, even by the standard of wealth set in Paris. She was a sportswoman and, despite her lack of frailty, had led an outdoor life and possessed a nerve of steel.

Madame de Warens had brought the girl up after she left school, had laboured over her and found her labour in vain. Cléo had no leanings towards the People and the opinions of her aunt seemed to her a sort of disreputable madness bred on hypocrisy. Cléo looked on the lower classes just as she looked on animals, beings with rights of their own but belonging to an entirely different order of creation, and one thing certainly could be said for her—she was honest in her outlook on life.

Beside her sat Doctor Epinard, the ship's doctor, a serious young man who spoke little, and the fifth at table was Lagross, the sea painter, who had come for the sake of his health and to absorb the colours of the ocean. The vision of the *Albatross* with towering canvas breasting the blue-green seas in an atmosphere of sunset and storm was with him still as he sat listening to the chatter of the others and occasionally joining in. He intended to paint that picture.

It had come to him as a surprise. They had been playing cards when a quarter-master called them on deck saying that the weather had moderated and that there was a ship in sight, and there, away across the tumbling seas, the *Albatross* had struck his vision, remote, storm surrounded, and sunlit, almost a vision of the past in these days of mechanism.

"Now tell me, Prince," Madame de Warens was saying, "how long do you propose staying at this Kerguelen Land of yours?"

"Not more than a week," replied the Prince. "I want to take some soundings off the Smoky Islands and I shall put in for a day on the mainland where you can go ashore if you like, but I shan't stay here long. It is like putting one's head into a wolf's mouth."

"How is that?"

"Weather. You saw that sudden squall we passed through this evening, or rather you heard it, no doubt, well that's the sort of thing Kerguelen brews."

"Suppose," said the astute old lady, "it brewed one of those things, only much worse, and we were blown ashore?"

"Impossible."

"Why?"

"Our engines can fight anything."

"Are there any natives in this place?"

"Only penguins and rabbits."

"Tell me," said Lagross, "that three-master we saw just now, would she be making for Kerguelen?"

"Oh, no, she must be out of her course and beating up north. She's not a whaler, and ships like that would keep north of the Crozets. Probably she was driven down by that big storm we had a week ago. We wouldn't be where we are only that I took those soundings south of Marion Island."

"And, after Kerguelen, what land shall we see next?" asked the old lady.

"New Amsterdam, madame," replied the Prince, "and after that the Sunda Islands and beautiful Java with its sun and palm trees."

Mademoiselle de Bromsart shivered slightly. She had been silent up to this, and she spoke now with eyes fixed far away as if viewing the picture of Java with its palms and sapphire skies.

"Could we not go there now?" asked she.

"In what way?" asked the Prince.

"Turn the ship round and leave this place behind," she replied.

"But why?"

"I don't know," said she, "perhaps it is what you say about Kerguelen, or perhaps it was the sight of that big ship all alone out there, but I feel—" she stopped short.

"Yes—"

"That ship frightened me."

"Frightened you," cried Madame de Warens, "why, Cléo, what is the matter with you tonight? You who are never frightened. I'm not easily frightened, but I admit I almost said my prayers in that storm, and you, you were doing embroidery."

"Oh, I am not frightened of storms or things in the ordinary way," said the girl half laughing. "Physical things have no power over me, an ugly face can frighten me more than the threat of a blow. It is a question of psychology. That ship produced on my mind a feeling as though I had seen desolation itself, and something worse."

"Something worse!" cried Madame de Warens, "what can be worse than desolation?"

"I don't know," said Cléo, "It also made me feel that I wanted to be far away from it and from here. Then, Monsieur le Prince, with his story of desolate Kerguelen, completed the feeling. It is strong upon me now."

"You do not wish to go to Kerguelen then?" said the Prince smiling as he helped himself to the entrée that was being passed round.

"Oh, monsieur, it is not a question of my wishes at all," replied the girl.

"But, excuse me," replied the owner of the *Gaston de Paris*, "it is entirely a question of your wishes. We are not a cargo boat, Captain Lepine is on the bridge, he has only to go into his chart house, set his course for New Amsterdam, and a turn of the wheel will put our stern to the south." He touched an electric bell push, attached to the table, as he spoke.

"And your soundings?" asked she.

"They can wait for someother time or someother man, sea depths are pretty constant."

A quarter-master appeared at the saloon door, came forward and saluted.

"Ask Captain Lepine to come aft," said the Prince. "I wish to speak to him."

"Wait," said Mademoiselle Bromsart. Then to her host. "No. I will not have the course altered for me. I am quite clear upon that point. What I said was foolish and it would pain me more than I can tell to have it acted upon. I really mean what I say."

He looked at her for a moment and seemed to glimpse something of the iron will that lay at the heart of her beauty and fragility.

"That will do," said he to the quarter-master. "You need not give my message."

Madame de Warens laughed. "That is what it is to be young," said she, "if an old woman like me had spoken of changing our course I doubt if your quarter-master would have been called, Monsieur. But I have no fads and fancies, thank heaven, I leave all that to the young women of today."

"Pardon me, madame," said Doctor Epinard speaking for almost the first time, "but in impressions produced by objects upon the mind there is no room for the term fancy. I speak of course of the normal mind free of disease. Furthermore, we talk of objects as things of secondary importance and the mind as everything. Now I am firmly convinced that the mind of man, so far from being a thing apart from the objects that form its environment, is, in fact, nothing else but a mirror or focus upon which objects register their impressions and that all the thinking in the world is done not really by the mind but by the objects that form our thoughts and the reasons, utterly divorced from what we call human reason, that connect together the objects that form our environment."

"Is this a theory of your own, Epinard?" asked the Prince.

"It is, monsieur, and it may be bad or good but I adhere to it."

"You mean to say that man is composed entirely of environment, past and present?"

"Yes, monsieur, you have caught my meaning exactly. Past and present. Man is nothing more than a concretion formed from emanations of all the objects whose emanations have impinged upon living tissue since, at the beginning of the world, living tissue was formed. He is the sunset he saw a million years ago, the water he swam in when he was a fish, the knight in armour he fought with when he was an ancestor, or rather he is a concretion of the light, touch and sound vibrations from these and a million other things. I have written the matter fully out in a thesis, which I hope to publish some day."

"Well, you may put my name down for a dozen copies," said the Prince, "for certainly the theory is less mad than some of the theories I have come across explaining the origin of mind."

"But what has all that to do with the ship?" asked Madame de Warens.

"Simply, madame, that the ship which one looked at as a structure of canvas and wood, once seen by Mademoiselle de Bromsart, has become part of her mind, just as it has become part of yours and mine, a logical and definite part of our minds; now, mark me, there was also the sunset and the storm clouds, those objects also became part of the mind of Mademoiselle de Bromsart, and the reasons interlying between all these objects produced in her a definite and painful impression. They were, in fact, all thinking something which she interpreted."

"It seemed to me," said the girl, "that I saw Loneliness itself, and for the first time, and I felt just now that it was following me. It was to escape from that absurd phantom that I suggested to Monsieur le Prince that we should alter our course."

"Well," said Madame de Warens, "your will has conquered the Phantom. Let us talk of something more cheerful."

"Listen!" said Mademoiselle de Bromsart. "It seems to me that the engines are going slower."

"You have a quick ear, mademoiselle," said the Prince, "they undoubtedly are. The Captain has reduced speed. Kerguelen is before us, or rather on our starboard bow, and daybreak will, no doubt, give us a view of it. We do not want to be too close to it in the dark hours, that is why speed has been reduced."

Coffee was served at table and presently, amidst the fumes of cigarette smoke, the conversation turned to politics, the works of Anatole France, and other absorbing subjects. One might have fancied oneself in Paris but for the vibrations of the propeller, the heave of the sea, and the hundred little noises that mark the passage of a ship under way.

Later Mademoiselle de Bromsart found herself in the smoking-room alone with her host, Madame de Warens having retired to her state-room and the others gone on deck.

The girl was doing some embroidery work which she had fetched from her cabin and the Prince was glancing at the pages of the Revue des Deux Mondes. Presently he laid the book down.

"I was in earnest," said he.

"How?" she asked, glancing up from her work.

"When I proposed altering the course. Nothing would please me more than to spoil a plan of my own to please you."

"It is good of you to say that," she replied, "all the same I am glad I did not spoil your plan, not so much for your sake as my own."

"How?"

"I would rather die than run away from danger."

"So you feared danger?"

"No, I did not fear it, but I felt it. I felt a premonition of danger. I did not say so at dinner. I did not want to alarm the others."

He looked at her curiously for a moment, contrasting her fragility and beauty with the something unbendable that was her spirit, her soul—call it what you will.

"Well," said he, "your slightest wish is my law. I have been going to speak to you for the last few days. I will say what I want to say now. It is only four words. Will you marry me?"

She looked up at him, meeting his eyes full and straight.

"No," said she, "it is impossible."

"Why?"

"I have a very great regard for you—but—"

"You do not love me?"

She said nothing, going on with her work calmly as though the conversation was about some ordinary topic.

"I don't see why you should," he went on, "but look around you—how many people marry for love now-a-days—and those who do, are they any the happier? I have seen a very great deal of the world and I know for a fact that happiness in marriage has little to do with what the poets call love and everything to do with companionship. If a man and woman are good companions then they are happy together, if not they are miserable, no matter how much they may love one another at the start."

"Have you seen much of the world?" she raised her eyes again as she asked the question. "Have you seen anything really of the world? I do not mean to be rude, but this world of ours, this world of society that holds us all, is there anything real about it, since nearly everything in it is a sham? Look at the lives we lead, look at Paris and London and Berlin. Why the very language of society is framed to say things we do not mean."

"It is civilization. How else would you have it?"

"I don't know," she replied, "but I do know it is not life. It is dishonesty. You say that the only happy married people are those that are good companions, that love does not count in the long run, and you are right, perhaps, as far as what you call the World is concerned. I only repeat that the thing you call the World is not the real world, for love is real, and love is not merely a question of good companionship. It is an immortal bond between two spirits and death cannot break it."

"You speak as though you were very certain of a thing which, of all things, is most hidden from us."

"I speak by instinct."

"Well," said the Prince, "perhaps you are right. We have left behind us the simplicity of the old world, we have become artificial, our life is a sham—but what would you have and how are we to alter it? We are all like passengers in a train travelling to heaven knows where; the seats are well cushioned and the dining-car leaves nothing to be desired, but I admit the atmosphere is stuffy and the long journey has developed all sorts of unpleasant traits among the passengers—well, what would you do? We cannot get out."

"I suppose not," said she.

He rose up and stood for a moment turning over some magazines lying on the table. He had received his answer and he knew instinctively that it was useless to pursue the business further.

Then after a few more words he went on deck. The wind had fallen to a steady blow but the sky was still overcast and the atmosphere was heavy and clammy and not consistent. It was as though the low lying clouds dipped here and there to touch the sea. Every now and then the *Gaston de Paris* would run into a wreath of fog and pass through it into the clear darkness of the night beyond.

In the darkness aft of the bridge nothing could be seen but the pale hint of the bridge canvas and a trace of spars and funnels now wiped out with mist, now visible again against the night.

The Prince leaned on the weather rail and looked over at the tumble and sud of the water lit here and there with the gleam of a port light.

Cléo de Bromsart had fascinated him, grown upon him, compelled him in some mysterious way to ask her to marry him. He had sworn after his disastrous first experience never to marry again. He had attempted to break his oath. Was he in love with her? He could scarcely answer that question himself. But this he knew, that her refusal of him and the words she had said were filling his mind with quite new ideas.

Was she right after all in her statement that he who fancied himself a man of the world knew nothing of the world except its shams? Was she right in her statement that love was a bond between two spirits, a bond unbreakable by death? That old idea was not new to him, he had played with it as a toy of the mind constructed for the mind to play with by the poets.

The new thing was to find this idea in the mind of a young girl and to hear it expressed with such conviction.

After a while he came forward and went up the steps to the bridge. Captain Lepine was in the chart room, the first officer was on the bridge and Bouvalot, an old navy quarter-master, had the wheel.

"We have slowed down," said the Prince.

"Yes, monsieur," replied the first officer, "we are getting close to land. We ought to sight Kerguelen at dawn."

"What do you think of the weather?"

"I don't think the weather will bother us much, monsieur, that blow had nothing behind it, and were it not for these fog patches I would ask nothing better; but then it's Kerguelen—what can one expect!"

"True," said the other, "it's a vile place, by all accounts, as far as weather is concerned."

He tapped at the door of the chart room and entered.

The chart room of the *Gaston de Paris* was a pleasant change from the dark and damp of the bridge. A couch upholstered in red velvet ran along one side of it and on the couch with one leg up and a pipe in his mouth the captain was resting himself, a big man of the Southern French navy type, with a beard of burnt-up black that reached nearly to his eyes.

The Prince, telling him not to move, sat down and lit a cigar. Then they fell into talk.

Lepine was a sailor and nothing else. Had his character been cut out of cardboard the line of division between the sailor and the rest of the world could not have been more sharply marked. That was perhaps why the two men, though divided by a vast social gulf, were friends, almost chums.

They talked for half an hour or so on all sorts of subjects connected with the ship.

"By the way, Lepine," said the Prince suddenly, "It has been the toss up of a sou that we are not now steering a course for New Amsterdam."

"And how is that, monsieur?"

"Well, Mademoiselle de Bromsart proposed to me at dinner that we should alter our course, the idea came to her that some misfortune might happen to us off Kerguelen and, as you know, I am always anxious to please my guests—well, I called a quarter-master down. I was going to have sent for you."

"To alter our course?"

"Yes, but Mademoiselle de Bromsart altered her mind. She refused to let me send for you."

"But what gave the young lady that idea?" asked the Captain.

"That big ship we sighted before dinner."

"The three-master?"

"Yes, there was something about it she did not like."

"Monsieur, what an idea—and what was wrong with it?"

"Oh, it was just a fancy. The sea breeds fancies and superstitions, you know that, Lepine, for I believe you are superstitious yourself."

"Perhaps, monsieur; all sailors are, and I have had experiences. There are bad and good ships, just as there are bad and good men, of that I am sure. Perhaps that three-master was a bad ship." Lepine laughed as though at his own words. "All the same," he went on, "I don't like warnings, especially off Kerguelen."

They left the chart house and came out on the bridge.

The wind was still steady but the clouds had consolidated and the night was pitch black. On the bridge the *Gaston de Paris* seemed driving into a solid wall of ebony.

The Prince after a glance into the binnacle was preparing to go down the bridge steps when a cry from the Look-out made him wheel round. Suddenly, and as if evolved by magic from the blackness, the vague spectre of a vast ship shewed up ahead on the port bow making to cross their course. Thundering along under full canvas without lights and seemingly blind, she seemed only a pistol shot away.

Then the owner of the *Gaston de Paris* did what no owner ought ever to do: seeing Destruction and judging that by a bold stroke it might be out-leaped, he sprang to the engine room telegraph and flung the lever to full speed ahead.

IV

Disaster

L eft alone, Mademoiselle de Bromsart finished the all but completed piece of embroidery in her lap. It did not take her five minutes. Then she held up the work and reviewed it with lips slightly pursed, then she rolled it up, rose, and went off to the state-room of Madame de Warens to bid her goodnight.

Madame was sitting up in her bunk reading Maurice Barres' "Greco." The air of the place was stifling with the fume of cigarettes, and the girl nearly choked as she closed the door and stood facing the old lady in the bunk.

"Why don't you smoke, then you wouldn't mind it," cried the latter, putting her book down and taking off her glasses. "No, I won't have a port opened, d'you want me to be blown out of my bunk? Sit down."

"No, I won't stay," replied the other, "I just came to say goodnight— and tell you something—He asked me to marry him."

"Who—Selm?"

"Yes."

"And what did you say?"

"I said 'No.'"

"Oh, you did?—and what's the matter with him—I mean what's the matter with you?"

"How?"

"How! The best match in Europe and you say 'no' to him—a man who could marry where he pleases and whom he pleased and you say 'no.' Good-looking, without vices, richer than many a crowned head, second only to the reigning families—and you say 'no.'"

The old lady was working herself up. This admirer of Anarchasis Clootz and dilletanti of Anarchism had lately possessed one supreme desire, the desire to have for niece the Princess Selm.

"I thought you didn't believe in all that," said the girl.

"All what?"

"Titles, wealth and so forth."

"I believe in seeing you happy and well-placed. I was not thinking of myself—well, there, it's done. There is no use in talking anymore, for I know your disposition. You are hard, mademoiselle, that is your failing—without real heart. It is the modern disease. Well, that is all I have to say. I wish you goodnight."

She put on her spectacles again.

"Goodnight," said the other.

She went out, closed the door, and entered her state-room.

It was the same as Madame de Warens' only larger, a place to fill the mind of the old-time seafarers with the wildest surprise, for here was everything that a mortal could demand in the way of comfort and nothing of the stuffy upholstery that the word "state-rooms" suggests to the mind of the ordinary traveller.

The crimson velvet, so dear to the heart of the ship furnisher, was supplanted by ribbed silk, Persian rugs covered the floor, the metal fittings were of bronze, and worked, where possible, into sea designs: dolphins, sea-horses, and fucus. There was a writing-table that could be closed up into the wall so cunningly that no trace was left of where it had been, a tiny library of slim volumes uniformly bound in amber leather, a miracle of binding, the work of Grossart of Tours, a map-rack containing large scale maps of the world, and a tell-tale compass shewing the course of the *Gaston de Paris* to whomever cared to read it. A long mirror let into the bulkhead aft increased the apparent size of the place. A bath-room and dressing-room lay forward.

Having closed the door she stood for a moment glancing at her reflection in the mirror. The picture seemed to fascinate her as though it were the reflection of some stranger. Then, turning from the mirror, she sat down for a moment on the couch by the door.

She felt disturbed. The words of Madame de Warens had angered her, producing the effect of a false accusation to which one is too proud to reply, but the momentary anger had passed, giving place to a craving for freedom and fresh air. The atmosphere of the state-room felt stifling, she would go on deck. Then she remembered that she was in a thin evening dress and that she would have to change.

The two women shared a maid, and she was in the act of stretching out her hand to the electric bell by the couch to summon the maid, when the craving to get on deck without delay became so strong that she rose, went into the dressing-room and, without assistance, changed her gown for a tweed coat and skirt and her thin evening shoes for a pair of serviceable boots. Then she slipped on her oilskin and sou'wester and coming back into the state-room caught a momentary glimpse of herself in the mirror, a strange contrast to the elegant and black-gowned figure that had glanced at its reflection only ten minutes before.

She was coming up the saloon companion-way when the engines, easily heard from here, suddenly began a thunderous pow-wow; the ship lurched forward, and from the blackness of the open hatch above came a voice like the sudden clamour of sea-gulls. Then she was flung backwards and stretched, half-stunned, on the mat at the companion-way foot.

For a moment she did not know in the least what had happened. She fancied she had slipped and fallen, then, as she scrambled on to her hands and knees, someone passed her, nearly treading on her, and rushed up the companion-way to the deck. It was the chief steward. Rising and holding on to the rail she followed him.

The deck was aslant, and in the windy blackness of the night nothing was to be seen for a moment; but the darkness was terrific with voices, voices from forward of the bridge and voices from alongside as though a hundred drunken sailors were yelling and blaspheming from a quay.

For the tenth of a second the idea of being alongside a quay came to her with nightmare effect, heightened by a ruffling and booming from the sky above, a rippling and flapping and thundering like the sound of vast and tangled wings.

Then a blaze of light shot out, making day.

The arc lamp of the fore-mast, always ready to be used for night work, had been run up and switched on.

To starboard and stern of the *Gaston de Paris*, a great ship, within pistol shot of the deck, and with her canvas spilling the wind and thrashing and thundering, was dipping her bows in the sea. Men were fighting for the boats, and the stern was so high that more than half of the rudder shewed like a great door swinging on its hinges. On the counter in pale letters the word

"Albatross"

shewed, and to the mind of the gazer all the horror seemed focussed in that calm statement, those commonplace letters written upon destruction.

Clinging to the hatch combing she saw, now, as a person sees in a dream, sailors rushing and struggling aft along the slanting main deck. The engines had ceased working but the dynamos were running

HENRY DE VERE STACPOOLE

on steam from the main boilers, and through the noises that filled the night the sewing machine sound of them threshed like a pulse. What had happened, what was happening, she did not know. The great ship to port seemed sinking but the *Gaston de Paris* seemed safe, but for the horrible slant of the decks; she called out to the sailors, now clustered here and there by the boat davits, but her voice blew away on the wind, she saw Prince Selm, he was struggling aft along the slippery sloping deck, clutching at the bulwarks as he came, he seemed like a man engaged in some fantastic game—an unreal figure, now he was on the deck on all fours, now up again, clutching men by the shoulders, shaking them, shouting. She could hear his voice. The starboard boats were unworkable owing to the list to port. She did not know that, she only knew, and now for the first time, that the *Gaston de Paris* was in fearful danger. And instantly the thought came to her of the old woman below in her bunk and, on the thought, the mad instinct to rush below and save her.

Holding on to the woodwork of the hatch she was crawling towards the opening when blackness hit her like a blow between the eyes. The arc lamp had gone out, the dynamos had ceased running.

On the stroke of the darkness the *Gaston de Paris* heeled slightly deeper, flinging her to her knees, and as she hung, clutching the woodwork, she heard her name.

It was the Prince's voice. She answered, and at once on her answer a hand seized her cruelly as a vice. It caught her by the shoulder. She felt herself dragged along, buffeted, lifted, cast down—then nothing more.

V

Voices in the Night

The boat tackle of the *Gaston de Paris* was the latest patent arrangement for lowering boats in a hurry; every boat was provisioned, and the water casks left nothing to be desired, there were frequent inspections and boat drills. Yet when the *Gaston de Paris* foundered only three souls were saved.

The starboard boats, owing to the list, could not be lowered at all; every boat had its canvas cover on, which did not expedite matters. The patent tackle developed defects in practise, and, to crown all, the men panicked owing to the sudden darkness that fell on them like a clap on the extinction of the electric light. The port quarter-boat into which the girl had been flung had two men in her and was lowered away by Prince Selm, the doctor and the first officer; panic had herded the rest of the hands towards the pinnace and forward boats, and the pinnace, over-crowded, was stoved by the sea as soon as she was water-bourne. The other boats never left their davits, they went with the ship when the decks opened and the boilers saluted the night with a column of coloured steam and a clap of thunder that resounded for miles.

The whole tragedy from impact to explosion lasted only seven minutes.

The two men in the boat with the girl had shoved off like demons and taken to the oars as soon as the falls were released. If they had not, being so short-handed for the size of the boat, they would have been stoved; as it was they were nearly wrecked by a balk of timber from the explosion. It missed them by a short two fathoms, drenching them with spray, and then the night shut down pierced by voices, voices of men swimming and crying for help.

The rowers did not know each other. The bow oar shouted to the stern. "Is that you Larsen?"

"No, Bompard, and you?"

"La Touche—Row—God! Listen, there's a chap ahead."

The cries ahead ceased, and the boat bumped on something that duddered away under it and sank.

"He's gone, whoever he is," cried Bompard. "No use hunting for him. Listen, there's more." Voices shrill and voices bubbling came through the blackness from here and from there. The men tried to locate them and rowed now in this direction, now in that—always wrong. Once a voice sudden and shrill and close to the boat cried "A moi," and at the same instant Bompard's oar struck something, but they found nothing, the voice had ceased.

They could see, now, the waves like spectres evolving themselves from the night, a vision touching the very limit of dimness, and now as they entered a mist patch—nothing. The voices to port and starboard were ceasing, one by one—being blotted out. Then silence fell, broken only by the sound of the oars. La Touche shouted and shouted again, but there came no response. Then came Bompard's voice. "Is that hooker gone, too?"

"Curse her, yes. I was the lookout. Sailing without lights."

"This woman seems dead."

"It's the girl. I heard her squeal out as they hove her in. Let her lie. Well, this is a start."

"A black job, but we're out of it, so far."

"Ay, as far as we've got—as far as we've got. Well, there's no use rowing, there's no sea to hurt her, let her toss."

The oars came in and the fellows slithered from their seats on to the bottom boards. Ballasted so the boat rode easy. They lay like shivering dogs, grumbling and cursing and then, as they lay, the talk went on.

"Mon Dieu! What a thing—but we've grub and water all right."

"Ay, the boats are all right for that."

There was a long silence and then La Touche began in a high complaining voice:

"I was lookout, but it was not my fault, that I swear. I saw nothing till a big three-master broke out of the smother making to cross our bows, no lights shewing, snoring along asleep. Then I shouted. The bridge had seen her too and put the engines full speed ahead. They'd mistaken the distance, thought to clear her. I got aft. Hadn't reached the port alley way when the smash came. It was all the fault of those fools on the bridge."

"Who knows," came Bompard's voice. "Things happen and what is to be must be. Well, they're all gone a hundred fathoms deep and here we are drifting about with a dead woman. I'd sooner have any other cargo if I was given my choice."

"Sure she's dead?"

"Ay, she's dead sure enough by the way she's lying, not a breath in her."

Neither man suggested that she should be cast over. She ballasted the boat, and for Bompard she was something to lean against.

The French mercantile marine is divided into two great classes, the northerners and southerners. The man from the north is a Ponantaise, the man from the south a Moco.

Bompard was a Moco, La Touche a Ponantaise. They talked and talked, repeating themselves, cursing the "hooker," the Bridge and the steersman. Once La Touche, grown hysterical, seemed choking against tears.

Then after a while, conversation died out. They had nothing more to talk about. The boat rode easy. There was nothing to do, and these men blunt to life and sea-hardened so that to them all things came in the hour's work, nodded off, La Touche curled up in the bow, Bompard with his grizzled head on the breast of Mademoiselle de Bromsart.

VI

DAWN

The girl was not dead as Bompard imagined, she had been stunned and had passed from that condition into the pseudo-sleep that follows profound excitement.

She was awakened by a flick of spray on her face, a touch from the great sea that had claimed her for its own.

Lying as she was she could see nothing but the ribbed sides of the boat, the grey sky above, and a gull with domed wings and down-curved head, poised, as though suspended on the end of a string. It screamed at her, shifted its position, and then passed, as though blown away on the wind. She sat up. Bompard had drawn away from her and was lying curled up on his side. La Touche on his back, forward, shewed nothing but his knees; across the gunnel lay the sea, desolate in the dawn, turbulent, yet hard and mournful as a view of slated roofs after rain.

She had never seen the sea so close before, she had never smelt its heart and the savour of its soul; bitter, fresh, new and ever renewed by the blowing wind.

The whole tragedy of the night was alive in her mind as a picture, but it seemed the picture of what another person had seen. Her past life, her own personality, seemed vague and unconnected with her as the past life and personality of another person. This was reality. Reality new, terrific, pungent as that which the soul may experience on awakening after death.

She knew, as though the desolate sea had told her, that the great yacht was gone and everyone on board of her; yet the fact, perhaps from its very enormity, failed to realize itself fully in her mind. Then, in a flash and horribly clearly, came the picture of her immediate environment on board the *Gaston de Paris*, quite little things and things more important: the silver-plated taps of the bath in the bath-room, adjoining her cabin, the silk curtains of her bunk, the hundred and one trifles that made for comfort and ease. She saw the cabin servants and the face of the chief steward, a fat pale-faced man, a typical *maître d'hôtel*; the dinner of the night before, when the people seemed to her phantoms and the food, table equipage, knives, forks and spoons, realities.

All these things stood forth against the blankness and desolation of the sea, the sea she could touch by dipping her hand over the gunnel, the sea that had stripped her of everything but life and body, the dress and boots she wore and the yellow oilskin coat that covered her. Her hand resting on the gunnel shewed her that she still wore her rings, exquisite rings of emerald, ruby and diamonds, fresh washed with spray. They held her eyes as her mind, swaying just as the boat swayed to the swell, tried to re-construct yesterday and to feel.

Horror, pity for the fate of the others, the sense of the great disaster that had happened to the *Gaston de Paris*, of these only the latter possessed any vitality in her mind. The feeling of unreality destroyed her grip upon all else.

Her mind was subdued to her own condition. The hard angles of the woodwork against which she leaned and the spray upon her face, the boat and the men in it, the sharp cut wave tops—these were real, with an appalling reality.

It was as though she had never come across a real thing before, and across her mind came a vague, vague recognition of that great truth that real things bruise one, eat at one, try to make one their own, once they manage to break down the barrier of custom that separates the false from the true; that quite common things have a power greater than the power of mind, that only amidst the falsity of civilised life and the stage are the properties subordinate to the persons and emotions of the actors.

At this moment Bompard, suddenly moving in his sleep, roused himself and sat up. His rough, weather beaten face was expressionless for a moment, then his eyes fell on the girl and recognition seemed to come to him.

"Mon Dieu," cried the old fellow as if addressing some unseen person. "'Tis all true then—" Then, as though remembering something—"but how is mademoiselle alive?"

"I don't know," said the girl, unconscious as to what he was referring to. "I know you, I have seen you often on deck—who is the other man? Oh, is it possible that we are the only people left?"

Bompard, without replying, swung his head round, then he rose and came over the thwarts. He caught La Touche by the leg.

"Gaston—rouse up—the lady is alive. It's me. Bompard."

La Touche sat up, his hair towsled, his face creased, he seemed furious about something and pushing Bompard away stared round and round at sea and sky as if in search of someone.

HENRY DE VERE STACPOOLE

"Bon Dieu," cried La Touche. "The cursed boat." He spat as though something bitter were in his mouth and wiped his lips with the back of his hand. He did not seem to care a button whether the lady were alive or not. He had been dreaming that he was in a tavern, just raising a glass to his mouth, and Bompard had awakened him to this.

The girl could not repeat the question to which there seemed no answer, she crawled into the stern sheets and sitting there, half bent, watched the two men. An observer perched in the sky above might have noticed the curious fact that on board the forsaken boat quarter deck and fo'c'sle still held sway, that the lady was the lady and the hands the hands, that Bompard was talking in an undertone, saying to La Touche: "Come, get alive, get alive," and that La Touche, after his first outburst, was holding himself in. They were old yachtsmen, no disaster could shake that fact.

La Touche, rising and taking his seat on a thwart and looking everywhere but in the direction of the girl, as though ashamed of something, began cutting up some tobacco in a mechanical way, whilst Bompard, on his knees, was exploring the contents of the forward locker. La Touche was a fair-haired man, younger than Bompard, a melancholy looking individual who always seemed gazing at the worst of things. He spoke now as the girl drew his attention to something far away in the east, something sketched vaguely in the sky as though a picture lay there beyond the haze.

"Ay, that's Kerguelen," said La Touche.

Bompard, on his knees, and with a maconochie tin in his left hand, raised his head and looked.

"Ay, that's Kerguelen," said Bompard.

"And look," said the girl, pointing towards Kerguelen. "Is not that the sail of a boat, away ever so far—or is it a gull? Now it's gone. Look, there it is again."

Bompard looked.

"I see nothing," said he, "gull, most like   there wouldn't be any boat from us, they're all gone, unless it was a boat from that hooker we struck."

"Boat," said La Touche with a dismal laugh. "She got no boat away, she went down by the bows with the fellows like flies on her, this is the only boat of the lot that got away."

The girl with her hand shading her eyes was still looking.

"It's gone, whatever it may have been," said she, "can we reach the land?"

"Why, yes, mademoiselle," said Bompard, "the wind is setting towards there and we have a sail, I am going to step the mast now when I've taken stock—well, we won't starve. The tube is provisioned for a full crew for a fortnight, water too, we won't starve, that's a fact. La Touche, get a move on and help me with the sail."

"I'm coming," grumbled La Touche.

It seemed to the girl that the minds and the tongues and the movements of the two men were part of some slow-acting, wooden, automatic mechanism. Whether they reached the land or not seemed a matter almost of indifference to them. Accustomed to people who talked much and had much to talk about she could not understand. All this was part of the new world in which she found herself, part of the boat itself, of the mast, now stepped against the grey sky, the waves, the gulls, and that tremendous outline of mountains now more visible to the east— Kerguelen. A world of things without thought, or all but thoughtless, things that, yet, dominated mind more profoundly than the power of mind itself.

Bompard was munching a biscuit he had taken from one of the bread bags as he worked. She noticed the bag, its texture, and the words "Traversal—Toulon" stamped on it. The maconochie tin which he had placed on a seat and a tin of beef with a Libby label held her eyes as though they were things new and extraordinary. They were. They were food. She had never seen food before, food as it really is, the barrier between life and death, food naked and stripped of all pretence.

Bompard coming aft with the sheet shipped the tiller, and, taking his seat by the girl, put the boat before the wind. La Touche, who had taken his seat on the after thwart, was engaged in opening the tin of beef. The girl scarcely noticed him. She was experiencing a new sensation, the sensation of sailing with the wind and the run of the swell. The boat, from a dead thing tossing on the waves, had suddenly become a thing alive, buoyant, eager and full of purpose, silent, too, for the slapping and buffeting of the water against the planking had ceased. Running thus with the wind and swell there was no opposition, everything was with her.

"Well, it's beef," said La Touche who had managed to open the Libby tin, "it might be worse."

He dug out a piece with his knife and presented it to the girl with a biscuit, then he helped Bompard and himself, then he scrambled forward, leaving his beef and biscuit on the thwart, and reappeared with a pannikin of water; it was handed to the lady first.

The food seemed to loose their tongues. It was as though the caste difference had been broken by the act of eating together.

"I'd never thought to set tooth in a biscuit again when that smash came last night," said Bompard addressing no one in particular.

"I wasn't thinking of biscuits," said La Touche, "I was bowled over in the alley-way. You see, I was running, so it took me harder. What set me running I don't know, my legs took care of themselves—I was just leaning like this, see, on the look out and between two blinks there was the hooker crossing our course or making that way. She'll clear us, maybe, said I to myself, then the engines went full speed and I knew we were done. Then I cleared aft, running, with no thought in my mind but to get out of the way, dark, too, but I didn't barge against nothing, till the smash came, and I went truck over keel in the alley-way."

"I was coming up the cabin stairs," said Cléo, "and something seemed to knock me down. Then when I got on deck the light was put on and I saw a great ship on the right hand side; she seemed sinking, but I read her name, she was quite close. Then the light went out and someone caught me and threw me—I don't know where, but it must have been into this boat."

"That was it," said Bompard, talking and eating at the same time, "us two was in the boat."

"I thought it was Larsen," cut in La Touche. "Larsen helped me to get the canvas off her, that was when the electric was on—what became of Larsen?"

"Lord knows," said Bompard. "I scrambled into her just as the light was shut off, then the chaps on deck chucked the lady in. Next thing we were fending her off from the ship. I was shouting to the chaps on deck to jump and we'd pick them up, we'd got the oars out then. I tell you I was fuddled up for I'd got it in my head that the hooker was to port of us though I'd seen her with my own eyes to starboard. I was thinking we'd be taken down with the suck of her and I was bent on getting ahead of her."

"I didn't hear you shouting to the fellows on deck," said La Touche, "but I heard you shouting to me to row. Then when we'd got her away a bit the *Gaston* blew up."

"Blew up," said the girl.

"The boilers," said Bompard, "they lifted the decks off her. She must have gone like a stone."

"So you think no one at all escaped but us?"

Neither of the men replied for a moment, then La Touche said: "There wasn't another boat could have got away."

The sun was well risen now, the clouds were high and breaking and the far away land shewed up, vast in the distance, with a white line of snow-covered peaks against the sky, desolate as when Kerguelen first sighted them.

Cléo with her eyes fixed across the leagues of tumbling tourmaline tinted sea almost forgot the others. That was the place where the wind was bearing them to, a place where there was nothing. Neither hotels nor houses nor huts, nor men nor women, a place where no landing-stage would receive them, no voice welcome them. Her throat worked for a second convulsively as she battled with the quite new things that the far off mountains were telling her.

It was now and not till now that she recognised fully what Fate had done to her. It was now and not till now that she saw Time before her as a thing from which all the known features had been deleted.

"Mademoiselle's bath is quite ready."

"Mademoiselle, the first gong has sounded."

Oh, the day—the day with its hundred phases and divisions, the breakfast hour, the luncheon hour, the hour that brought afternoon tea, the dresses that went with each phase, the emotions and interests, and changing forms of being, the day which made a person change to its light and the person of ten o'clock in the morning quite different from the person of noon—this thing which we talk of as the day appeared before her now as what it really is, life itself, as civilized men know life, a thing outside ourselves yet of ourselves and without which the circling of the sun is as the circling of a pointer on a blank dial—. This thing was gone.

La Touche had got more forward and was smoking and, though the wind was with them, a faint scent of tobacco smoke came on the spill of the wind from the sail. Bompard was chewing, spitting occasionally to starboard and wiping his mouth with the back of his bronzed tattooed hand.

The vague scent of the tobacco threaded up all sorts of things in the girl's mind: Madame de Warens, the streets of Paris, the deck of the yacht. She remembered the piece of embroidery work she had been engaged on last night, and then a scrap of conversation she had overheard between the doctor and the artist towards the end of dinner, they were talking of the passéistes and futurists, of the work of Pablo Picasso, of Sunyer, of Boccioni and Durio, arguing with extraordinary passion about the work of these people.

"There's weather or something over there," said La Touche who had slipped down and was seated on the bottom boards with his back to a thwart; he nodded his head towards Kerguelen.

Around one of the highest peaks a lead-coloured cloud had wrapped itself turban-wise, and even as they looked the cloud turban increased in volume and height, mournful and monstrous as some djin-born vision of the Arabian story-tellers.

"That's snow," said Bompard, "and by the twist of it it's in a whirlwind."

"Bon Dieu, what a place," said La Touche.

"You may say that," said Bompard, "but that's nothing, it's when we come to make a landing we'll find what we are against."

"Oh, we've got so far we'll finish it," said La Touche.

Then began a dismal argument, full of words and repetitions but with few ideas, and from the trend of it the curious fact appeared that La Touche, the ship's grouser and dismal James, was taking the optimistical side, whilst Bompard, generally cheerful, was the pessimist.

La Touche's optimism was, perhaps, the outcome of fear. What they had gone through was nothing to the prospect of having to make a landing on that tremendous coast, simply because what they had gone through had come on them suddenly. This thing had to be faced in cold blood. The coward in La Touche refused to face it fully, refused to face the fact that with this swell and with all the chances of uncharted and unknown reefs and rocks the risk was appalling. He grew angry.

"Don't be a coward over it," said he. That set Bompard off, and for a moment the girl thought they would have come to blows. Then it passed and they were as friendly as before, just as though nothing had happened.

Their talk and the whole business had been conducted as though the girl were not there. In the few hours since daybreak, quarter deck and fo'c'sle had vanished. They had become welded into one community, all equal, and the lady was no longer the lady. There was no hint of disrespect, no hint of respect. They were all equal, equal sharers in the chances of the sea.

More, the sex standard seemed to have vanished with the social. Nothing remained but the human, for that is the rule with the open boat at sea.

When they lowered the sail for screening purposes, when they raised it again, it was all the same, for the human level is above all little things.

Towards noon and with the coast now closer and well-defined, La Touche sighted something ahead. It was a rock, high and pointed like a black spire protruding from the sea and standing there like an outpost of the land.

"Had we better give it a wide berth?" asked La Touche. "Maybe there's more near it."

"The sea is running smooth enough by it," said Bompard. "I don't see breakers, and we don't draw anything to speak of." He held on.

The sun was shewing through breaks in the high clouds and its light fell on the water and the rock, pied with roosting guillemots. As the boat drew near the guillemots gave tongue. The sound came against the wind fierce and complaining, antagonistic like the voice of loneliness crying out against them and telling them to be gone—be gone—be gone!

Cléo, as they passed, saw the green water sliding up and falling from the polished black rock surface. The sight seemed to bring the hostile coast leagues nearer and the bagpipe crying of the guillemots as it died away behind them seemed a barrier passed, never to be re-crossed.

VII

The Coast

A nd now, away at sea and leagues from the coast they were approaching, vast islands disclosed themselves suddenly through the sea haze, standing like giants waist deep in the ocean, whilst the coast itself with its cliffs and rocks of black basalt and dolerite shewed clear, extraordinarily clear, with every detail defined in the sunlight, from the rifts in the basalt to the gulls blowing about in legions and the great sea-geese hovering and fishing.

The coast was ferocious, and the whole country from the sea foam to the foothills looked tumbled and new, with the newness of infinite antiquity. The last thunders of creation seemed scarcely to have died away, the last throe scarcely to have ceased, leaving million-ton rock cast on rock and the new, shear-cut cliffs spitting back their first taste of the bitter sea.

"There is nowhere to land," said the girl. She was shuddering as a dog shudders when overstrung.

"Ay, it's a brute beast of a place," said Bompard, "well, we must nose along on the lookout. There's no coast but hasn't some landing-place where a boat can push in. Y'see it's not like a ship. A boat can go where a ship can't."

He shifted the helm a bit, keeping the coast parallel to them on the starboard side.

"Might those islands be better to go to?" asked she, "they couldn't be worse than that."

La Touche suddenly grew excited. "Bon Dieu," cried he, "what a thing to be saying! Those islands, nothing but rocks—nothing but rocks. Here there is land, at all events, good land one can put one's foot on; out there there's nothing but rocks. Rather than go out there I would swim ashore—I would—"

"Oh, close up," said Bompard, "don't talk about swimming—maybe you'll have to."

"One can always drown," said La Touche.

It was Bompard who next broke the silence.

"I've been over cliffs worse than those, for gulls eggs," said he, "take one coast with another, coasts are pretty much the same, you get bad bits and easy bits, that is all."

La Touche said nothing.

As they drew on the great islands out at sea ranged themselves more definitely and the tremendous coast to starboard shewed more clearly its deep cut canons, its sea arches and absolute desolation.

The sea had fallen, though the wind still held steady, and this surface calmness, under-run by a gentle swell, served only to emphasize the vastness of the view. The island seemed immensely remote and immense in size, the far snow-covered mountains the mountains of a land where giants had lived and from which they had departed countless ages ago.

Oyster catches passed the boat with their melancholy cry, but the fishing gannets and the swimming puffins seemed scarcely to heed the intruders. Puffins swimming a biscuit toss away as though they had never learned the fear of man.

They had drawn nearer shore so that the boom of the swell in the caves and on the rocks came to them with the crying of the shore birds; passing a headland like a vast lizard they opened a beach curved like the new moon and seven miles from horn to horn.

"There's our landing-place," cried Bompard, "big enough to pick and choose from."

"Lord!" shouted La Touche. "Look over there—moving rocks!"

He pointed half a mile away to seaward.

Bompard looked.

"Those crest rocks, they're whales," said he.

A pair of whales shewed, standing up, coupling in the chill blue grey water, a miraculous sight, as though they had entered a world where the original things of life still moved and had their being untroubled by man and untouched by Time.

Bompard shifted the helm, and the boat, heading for the shore and no longer running before the wind, moved less easily, shipping an occasional dash of spray.

The change of movement, the dash of spray, the altered course were to the girl like the turning of a corner. Running with the wind and with a parallel shore the boat was the world and the coast and island a panorama. With the twist of the helm Reality made the coast a destination. Up to this moment the uncertainty of whether they could land had held her mind, up to this moment all sorts of vague possibilities, the chance of meeting a ship, the chance of being blown out to sea, the chance of this or that had come between her and the realisation of the fact that this prison was hers.

The monstrosity of the idea stood fully revealed only now on that beach where there was nothing but sand, nothing but rocks, nothing but gulls. Close in now Bompard let go the sheet and they unstepped the mast, the boat rocking in the trough of the swell. Then they got the oars out.

As they bent to their work and over the creak of the leather in the rowlocks the rumble and fume of the seven mile beach came mixed with the yelping and mewing of the gulls. The boat made slow progress, then a few yards from the surf line it hung for a moment till the rowers suddenly gave way and moving like a relieved arrow she came on the crest of a wave, then the oars came in with a crash and the two men tumbling out dragged her nose high and dry. They helped the girl out and as they pulled the boat higher she stood, the wind flicking her oilskin coat about her and the spindrift blowing in her face.

PART II

VIII

The Awakening

The great beach of Kerguelen shews above tide mark long stretches where no sand is, only rock. Basalt planed and smoothed by the seas of countless ages, level as a ball-room floor and broken by rifts and pot holes, between tide marks these pot holes serve as traps for all sorts of sea creatures. Once the waves must have beaten right up to the low and broken basalt cliffs full of caves floored with sand, but volcanic action raising the beach has pushed the tide mark out leaving a shore varying in width from half a mile to a few hundred yards.

This is the breeding place of the sea elephant. Half way between the lizard point and the point further to the east a river comes down disembarging through three months; on the banks of this river is the seal nursery where in summer the young sea elephants tumble and play and take their swimming lessons, whilst the mothers lie on rocks and the fathers fish and hunt and fight in battles, the roaring of which resounds for miles. Here the penguins drill and hold councils and law courts and marry and get divorced and hold political meetings, here the rabbits play and the terns foregather, and here the winds that blow from everywhere but the east, hunt and yell and pile in winter a twenty foot sea that breaks in seven miles of thunder under seven miles of spray thick as the smoke of battle.

Duck and teal haunt the place and gulls of nearly every known kind snow it and flick it with movement. Yet above the thunder of the waves and the cries of the birds and the shouting of the winds when they blow, there hangs a silence—the silence of the remote and prehistoric. The living world of men seems cut off from here by far away doors and forever.

After supper they had explored the cave mouths in the cliff opposite to where the boat had beached. There were three caves just here. One was impracticable owing to water dripping from the roof, but the other two, floored with hard sand, were good enough for shelter. The men had stowed the provisions and themselves in the western mast giving the girl the other and the boat sail for a pillow.

It was old Bompard who thought of the latter. La Touche seemed to have no thought for anyone or anything but himself. He grumbled all the time during supper, grumbled at the fact that there was no stuff to make a fire with, that they had nothing warm to drink, that sometime soon their tobacco must run out. It seemed to Cléo as she lay with her head on the hard sailcloth and her body on the hard sand, covered with the oilskin coat which she had taken off to use as a blanket, that through the league long rumble of the surf she could hear him grumbling still. She did not care. Hard though the floor was she did not mind, she was chloroformed. Chloroformed by the air of Kerguelen. The air that fills the lungs with life, keeps a man going all day with an energy and buoyancy unknown elsewhere and then fells him with sleep.

She awoke when the whale birds had ceased crying, just after dawn, awoke fresh and new and full of life. She felt none of that troubled surprise which comes when the mind has to adjust itself to the new situation on awakening for the first time after a great disaster. It was as though her mind had already adjusted itself and discounted everything.

She rose up and leaving the oilskin coat and sou'wester on the floor of the cave came out on to the beach.

The fine weather still held and the day was strong, now lighting the beach, the sea, and the distant islands through a sky of high, grey eastward drifting clouds. The boat lay where it had been pulled up, the tide now coming in and legions of birds were flitting and blowing about and stalking on the sands as far as eye could reach.

She came to the cave where the men were. Bompard and La Touche lying on their backs might have been dead but for the sound of their snoring. Bompard was lying with his wrist across his eyes, La Touche with both hands beside him, clenched. The tins of beef and the bread bags shewed vaguely in the gloom behind them.

She stood for a moment watching them and then, turning, she came down to the boat lying high and dry on the sand. She was trying to realize, that on the morning of the day before yesterday at this hour she had been lying in her bunk on board the *Gaston de Paris*, to realize this and also the fact that her present position seemed scarcely strange.

She ought, so she told herself, to be astonished at what had happened and to be bewailing her fate, yet, looking back now over yesterday and the day before, everything seemed part of a level and logical sequence, almost like the events of a stormy day on board ship. The tragedy of the destruction of the *Gaston* only partly experienced could not be fully felt.

Standing by the boat she tried to realize it and failed, tried to grasp what she knew to be the horror and pity of it, and failed. She was neither hard nor insensible, she simply could not grasp it.

And her position here with two rough men, very little food and little chance of escape, how she would have pitied herself a few days ago could she have foreseen! Yet here, with the firm sands under her feet and the wind blowing in her face, reality, instead of hurting her as it had done in the boat on awakening yesterday morning, soothed her and reassured her. Everything seemed firm again and the fear that the ugly coast had raised in her mind had vanished.

She came along the beach looking at the gulls, turned over huge star-fish and picked up kelp ribbons to examine them. Half a mile or so from the cave she was about to turn back when her eye caught a strange appearance on the sea, hundreds and hundreds of moving points drawing in to the shore, white and black points like a shoal of fish only half submerged. It was a fleet of swimming birds.

She sat down on the sand to watch as they took the shore with a rush through the foam. Then, safely beached, the fleet became an army of penguins. She had seen pictures of penguins so she knew what they were and she had read Anatole France's "Penquin Island"—these, then, were the real things and she watched them fascinated as one who sees storyland taking visible and concrete form.

The penguins formed line, broke into companies, drilled a bit and then began to move up the beach.

The figure of the girl did not seem to disturb them in the least.

One company passed to the left, one to the right, whilst that immediately fronting her halted a few feet away and saluted her, bowing like little old-fashioned men in black swallow-tail coats and immaculate shirt fronts, little old-fashioned men with sharp quizzical eyes, polished, humorous, polite and entirely friendly.

The company on the right wheeled to examine her as did the company on the left, so that she found herself almost in a hollow square. Wherever she turned there were birds bowing to her or things in the semblance of birds, absolutely fearless, so close that she could have touched them had she carried a walking-stick.

She rose up to allow them to pass and they went on like mechanical things wound up and released, forming line again and seeming to forget her.

She remembered the guillemots and their rudeness and the way they had stormed and jeered at the boat—did all that mean more than the politeness and friendliness of the penguins? If she were lying dead would not the guillemots pass her without enmity and the penguins without friendliness, as indifferent to her fate as the wave of the sea on the blowing wind?

They would—as indifferent as the great islands standing out there in the distance, mauve and slate grey against the morning. As she came back along the beach her mind was battling with a problem that had suddenly risen. She had neither brush nor comb nor glass. Her hair was beautiful and she loved it. Her face was beautiful but she did not love it, it was herself, she could not view it from an independent standpoint, but she could view her hair almost as impartially as a dress and she loved it with the strange passion that women have for things of texture.

The hair of Cléo de Bromsart had been waited upon like a divinity by many a priestess in the form of a maid. It had been dressed and shampooed and treated by artists and adepts, the hours of brushing alone if put together would have made a terrific total. The result was perfection, and even now, after all she had gone through, it shewed scarcely disarrangement, lustrous and beautiful, dressed with artful simplicity in the Greek style and outlining the perfect curves of her head.

The wind was blowing now in gusto from the sea, but she scarcely noticed it as she walked, facing the problem that shipwreck had put before her, a problem the first of a long queue ranging from soap to a change of garments.

She was fighting it and at the same time battling with the strengthening wind when suddenly something sprang on her with the yell of a tiger and flung her on the sand, pinning her there.

IX

The Wooley

It was the wind. The Wooley, which is the fist of Kerguelen suddenly clenched and hitting out from the shoulder of the great islands now suddenly stormed about with foam and veiled in spray.

Half stunned, she twisted round, still lying but fronting it now with her arm protecting her face. The beach had loudened up in thunder from end to end but the yelling Wooley as it met the cliffs and howled inland almost drowned the thunder of the waves. Then it died down as suddenly as it had come, and the boom of the surf rose high, as the girl, gathering herself together, got up and struggled on.

She was no longer thinking of her hair. It was the first lesson of the school of Kerguelen. "Here you shall think of nothing but the moment, of the ground beneath your feet, of the bite you put in your mouth, of the rock that stands before you."

When she reached the cave with her petticoats thrusting about her she was met by the two men and as she came up to them La Touche was cursing the wind. The Wooley had all but blown him down too. He had got up sooner than Bompard and had received the full face of it "in the pit of the stomach." He seemed to look on it as a personal matter affecting him alone.

Even as he spoke a sudden calm fell, lasted for a moment, and was followed by a howl from inland.

At a stroke the wind had changed right round and was blowing now from the mountains. Here in the shelter of the cliffs they scarcely felt it but the shift had raised an appalling cross sea. Right away to the islands there was nothing but tumbling foam, waves standing up and fighting waves in a battle that spread for leagues.

"It's well for us we didn't fall in with this yesterday," said Bompard "a ship couldn't stand it."

"And what ship will ever poke her nose in here to take us off do you think?" asked La Touche. "This is what you get everyday of the week, if all accounts are true—this, and worse. I tell you we've come to the wrong place. There's no getting over it. We've come to the wrong place."

"Well, right or wrong, here we are," said Bompard "Mon Dieu! to hear you talk you'd think we'd come here on purpose—come, get a move on and let's have some grub."

He turned into the cave and they fetched out the can of beef they had opened yesterday, some biscuits, and a water breaker, and sitting at the cave mouth they ate just as the men of the Stone Age ate, with the palms of their hands for plates and their fingers for forks. They spoke scarcely at all. The ill-humor of La Touche seemed like a contagious disease, even Bompard, the imperturbable, seemed glum.

It was the girl who broke the strain.

Suddenly she began to speak as if giving voice to carefully thought out ideas. Yet what she said was absolutely spontaneous, the result of a quick, educated mind suddenly grasping the essentials of their position, suggestion breeding suggestion.

"There's no use in grumbling," said she. "That wind knocked me down as I was coming along the beach. I didn't grumble, and there is no use in thinking. I was thinking as I walked along that I had no brush and comb to do my hair with, you two have short hair and you can't imagine what it is to a person with long hair when they find themselves without a brush and comb. I was grumbling to myself about it when the wind knocked me down. I want just to tell you what is in my mind: we will die or go mad if we do not forget everything as much as we can and not think of tomorrow or yesterday or ships coming to take us off. We have to fight all sorts of things that don't care in the least for us and we have to work. Everything here is at work in its own way. Well, we must do as everything else does or die."

"It's easy to say work," said La Touche munching a biscuit, "but what is one to work at?"

"We want food for one thing, our provisions won't last forever."

"There's rabbits enough," said Bompard. "Remember those rabbits we saw running out on the beach last evening?"

"I can snare rabbits all right," said La Touche, "but where's the wire to make snares with—see—we're caught everywhere."

"Wait," said Bompard.

He got up and went down to the boat, hunted in one of the lockers and returned with a spool of wire.

He flung it at La Touche.

"There's your wire," said he.

Cléo's eyes brightened. The spool of wire seemed to her a fruit suddenly born from her words; she had accomplished something, it was perhaps the first real accomplishment in her life.

"Where did you get it from?" asked La Touche.

"The forward locker," replied Bompard.

"Are there any other things in the locker?" asked the girl.

"Oh, Mon Dieu, yes," replied the old fellow. "There's a lot of truck, but it's no use to us."

"Let's go and see," said Cléo. She rose up and came down the beach followed by the others. The wind from the mountains died away but the sea torment remained and, though the tide was beginning to ebb, the spray of the waves almost reached the boat.

It had been listed to one side by the Wooley but was undamaged and the forward locker was still open as it had been left by the careless Bompard.

It was one of the boats used for fishing and deep sea work, hence the contents of the locker.

The steel head of a two pronged fish spear, a fisherman's knife in its sheath with belt, a paternoster, invaluable for the fathoms of fishing line attached, a small American axe with the head vaselined, a canvas housewife with sail-needles, a few darning needles and some pack thread, and a number of odds and ends including some extra heavy lead sinkers.

Bompard looked on apathetically and La Touche stood with his hands in his pockets as the girl fished the things out one by one, placing them, some on the sands and some on the thwarts of the boat.

The things seemed to have no interest for the men. Accustomed all their lives to being looked after as far as shelter and food were concerned they seemed absolutely helpless in front of new conditions. Men are like that, especially men of the people, and when you read of Crusoes and their wonderful doings on desert islands you read Romance.

The quick, trained mind of the girl seemed to see clearly where they could scarcely see at all, she had imagination and she was a woman— that is to say a being more gifted than man, with prevision in affairs purely material.

Bompard did not see any use in the axe and said so. The girl, with her hand resting on the gunnel of the boat, stood like a housekeeper trying to explain to a mere male creature the use of some household implement.

"We will want a fire and an axe will chop wood," said she.

"Ay, and where are you to get the wood?" asked La Touche. "There's not a tree on this blasted place, nor the sign of one."

"Well, we'll have to look—there may be trees inland—there's sure to be bushes of some sort—anyhow we will take these things up to the cave, they will be safer there."

The baling tin of the boat caught her eye, she included it amongst her prizes.

This baling tin, like a psychological instrument, exhibited the mind of Bompard as though that said mind had been scooped out and placed in it.

To him it was a baling tin; here there were no boats to be baled out—where was the use of it?

To the woman it was a possible pot to boil things in if they could get a fire and things to boil.

She explained and Bompard saw the light. La Touche saw it, too, but promptly pointed out that they had no fire and nothing to boil. He seemed to find an odious satisfaction in the fact, a satisfaction which Bompard faintly reflected, and for a moment the girl seemed to glimpse in the two men a lethargy of mind almost unthinkable. A lethargy and laziness, mulish, and kicking at anything that disturbed it, that actually fought against betterment because betterment meant exercise of intellect and action.

She felt angry with them, just as a grown person feels angry with lazy children, and putting the belt with the knife round her waist and picking up some of her treasures she ordered the others to follow with the rest.

When they had been placed in the cave with the provisions, Bompard, after his great labours, cut himself some tobacco and La Touche lit his pipe. Then they sat down at their cave opening to smoke and rest themselves whilst the girl, who could not keep still, went back to the boat to explore the other lockers and see if by chance anything else of a useful nature might be found. The two men seated smoking at the cave mouth watched her as she went. She felt their eyes upon her and guessed that they were discussing her, but she did not mind.

The ceaseless activity of old Madame de Warens seemed to have descended on her through the air of Kerguelen. The will that Prince Selm had divined in her had been aroused; the surroundings seemed to call her to action from every side; the past and the future seemed phantoms before the tremendous and insistent present. Fate could perhaps have broken her spirit only in one way, by casting her upon the sordid. If she had been socially shipwrecked and thrown onto a Paris slum she might have gone under. Here where everything was clean, where the air was life, where nothing was sordid, she swam; here she was miraculously filled with a new energy and an extraordinary new interest as though she were peeping at things for the very first time.

The forward locker was now empty, she hunted in the others and discovered two more Maconochie tins that Bompard had overlooked, some cotton waste, a roll of thick copper wire and a bradawl.

She collected the lot and brought them up to the cave before which her companions were seated.

She handed them to La Touche, who, without getting up, leaned back and pushed them as far into the cave as he could reach, then he resumed his pipe whilst Cléo standing and shading her eyes looked away up and down the beach as though measuring its possibilities.

"I found a lot of things down there this morning before the tide was high," said she. "There were star-fish, big ones like what I have seen on the beach at Bordighera; the Italian people eat them. I'm sure there must be lots of food to be found here on the beach. Then there is a big break in the cliffs lower down that seems to lead inland. I think the best thing we can do is to start now and hunt about and see what we can find. You two can go inland, and I will go along the beach. It's absolutely necessary to find any sort of food, and wood to make a fire."

The smokers were disposed to argue.

Yes, it was quite true, one must look round, but there was grub enough for a month and there was plenty of time before them. Then La Touche began to argue about star-fish. He had never heard of people eating star-fish. If they were to be condemned to eat stuff like that it would be better to quit. One might have fancied from his tone that it was Cléo's fault that such a suggestion should be made.

Cléo listened patiently and Bompard sat evidently approving. It was almost as though the two were in league against her, just as children get in league against an adult who insists on unpleasant duties or uncongenial food.

But a will was at work stronger than theirs and presently, tapping out their pipes, they rose up. La Touche, at her direction, placed the new found Maconochie tins, the cotton waste, the bradawl and wire with the rest of the stores, far back in the cave, and then, following her, they lumbered along down the beach in the direction of the cliff break like two schoolboys after a governess.

The cliff break was a narrow gully piercing the basalt and bending upon itself; here they parted, the men striking up the gulley and the girl continuing her way along the beach.

"And be sure to look out for some wood," she cried after them, "any sort of wood."

"Ay, ay," said Bompard, "we'll be on the look out right enough."

Then they vanished and she pursued her way alone, picking up things as she went, turning over shells and thinking of her companions.

The wind had fanned up again to a strong breeze but the sound of the surf had fallen with the receding tide and the stretch of wet sand below high tide mark was strewn with huge kelp ribbons, masses of seaweed, shells, all empty, cuttle fish bones and the star-fish despised of La Touche.

Then she came upon something that gave her a grue, it seemed at first like a white rock, it was a skull. The skull of some enormous creature half-bedded in the sand just above the tide mark, possibly cast up in some storm. She thought it might be the skull of a whale and as she stood looking at it, suddenly, the desolation around came in upon her with the fact that she was absolutely alone.

Suppose the men lost their way—suppose that they never came back? The thought clutched her heart like a hand. To be here, alone, absolutely alone, forever!

For a moment panic seized her and the wild impulse came upon her to turn and run back to the cave. Then she mastered herself, fighting down the surging in her throat, and continuing her way steadily and with renewed strength. She had not cast the thought away, she had mastered it and as she went she contemplated it as a victor contemplates the dead body of an assailant.

Then she saw the penguins, she had not noticed them before, they were drawn up in long lines at the base of the cliff and the sight of them destroyed the desolation just as the skull had crystallized it around her.

A great pow-wow was going on amongst the penguins. Three birds, separate from the others, were standing, two facing one another bowing and discussing something, the third standing by, putting in a word now and then and now and then coming right between the disputants.

She watched them for awhile and then went on. She had no time to

HENRY DE VERE STACPOOLE

waste. The thought of coming back empty handed after all her talk to the men pursued her. She was looking for food and had found none—nothing but the star-fish.

The gulls evidently found plenty of food. But for a human being there seemed nothing, and as she went on and on the thought of what would happen when those tins in the cave were empty came at her just as the terror of finding herself alone had come, and this thought was not to be combated by an effort of will simply because it was born of Reason.

Her clear and practical mind saw starvation, over-leaped the slender food barrier that held hunger only a month away from them and wandered in a wilderness where nothing was.

She had reached the rock surface now that stretched away level and smooth, broken by cracks and pot holes and strewn here and there with weed. The cliffs had fallen away, giving a view of the broken country and the mountains with their snow-covered tops, immense, wrapped in distance under the dull grey day, remote, yet clearly defined in that air, crystal clear as the air of Iceland.

It was like looking at Silence herself, silence set off and explained by the beach noises, the sound of the surf, the calling of the terns, the mewing of the great white gulls.

She saw Kerguelen as it is, as it was, as it ever will be. Standing there alone she saw it for the first time in all its utter nakedness. If no food were to be found on the busy beach, what food could be found in that carved, silent, cruel land where not a single tree shewed in all the miles of desolation?

A stealthy scraping sound behind her made her wheel round.

Up from a rock pond which she had passed without examining had risen a crab, its body was not bigger than the two fists of a man put together, yet it moved standing high up like a spider on slender stilts that if stretched out would have measured four feet or more. She watched it with dilated eyes as it scrambled and hurried along, vanishing at last like a spectre in some cleft of the rock. There was something of a skeleton about it as well as something of a spider, it was like a caricature of food drawn by Famine. It made the whole beach hideous for a moment and it made the food hunter almost afraid to go on. She crushed the fear and went on, reaching a place where the rocks ceased and a broad level of sand stretched to where the rocks began again and further on the river ran down.

Where the sand met the further rocks a huge conical stone stood with a gull roosting on its top, and just as a person fixes on some object as the limit of his walk she determined to go as far as this stone and then turn back.

As she drew close to it the gull flapped its wings and flew away and she saw that the thing was not a stone but the figure-head of a ship, the form of a woman with ample breasts, broken and scarred by years of weather and stained with the droppings of gulls. The arms were gone, but the great face remained almost in its entirety staring away across the sands and the sea.

It had once worn a crown, but the crown was broken away all but a little bit on the left side of the head and it had an appearance of life that almost daunted the girl as she stood looking, watching it, and listening to the singing sound of the beach echoes and the mewing and crying of the gulls.

Then as she moved closer her foot struck on something half buried in the sand, it was a balk of timber, ships timber was all about, sanded over, and in places half uncovered. Here was firewood enough for twenty years. In the figure-head alone there was enough to supply their wants for a long time to come.

She sat down to rest on a projecting piece of this timber near the figure. Close up to it like this it lost its touch of life and became simply a block of wood, and from this point she could see the beach over which she had travelled stretching away and away to the Lizard Point with the foam breaking around it and flown about by the never-resting gulls.

She had come nearly three miles and she had found something worth finding by just keeping on.

She remembered the spectre crab. It had nearly turned her back empty-handed, but she had kept on and she registered that fact deeply in her mind, dwelling on it with a pleasure she had never felt before.

Then she fell to thinking of the ship that all this belonged to and the storm that must have driven it here. The weeds of the high tide mark did not come within ten feet of the wreckage, so the waves must have come a hundred feet or more beyond where she was sitting. Perhaps it was at night with all this coast roaring in the darkness and the wind yelling above the shouting of the waves. And all that must have happened years ago, to judge by the work of the weather on the once gaily painted woman and the depth the timbers had sunk in the sand.

She rose up, and before starting back she glanced inland towards the mountains across the broken country.

Then she shaded her eyes.

Beyond the fringe of the beach and amongst the high broken rocks stood a cross.

X

The Cross

The thing itself startled her less than the fact that she had not seen it before. It was as though it had been put up whilst she sat to rest.

It was so striking, so palpably evident that anyone coming along towards the figure-head as she had done must have been attracted by it. To verify this she walked a few yards away and even as she did so the cross vanished, shut out from sight by the rock to the left of it. Only from the point of view of the figure-head could it be seen.

It was as though the beach had tried to frighten her again.

She came towards it, noticing as she came the shortness of the arms. It was less a cross than a sign-post, a sign-post raised on a mound of small rocks; it was tarred to preserve it from the weather. From the left limb close to the post a metal box was hanging by a wire, and on the post itself, a few feet from the base, there was a plate of galvanised iron nailed to the wood. On the plate were stamped some words.

She stepped upon the mound and read: "Kestrel Expedition. Cache I. Don't disturb 19—"

The date was three years back.

The cache, whatever it might be, was under the mound. Also, this thing had evidently nothing to do with the wreck, for the embossed metal plate must have been prepared in some civilized country for the purpose to which it had been put.

She reached up and tried to detach the box and pulling on it brought down the slat of wood that formed the arms of the cross, the nails that had held it having rusted away.

Then, having detached the box, she examined it. It was an ordinary sailor's tobacco box, she pressed the spring, opened it, and found a piece of paper folded in four and inscribed as follows, the writing done with a purple indelible pencil:

> Opened the cach.
> Took nuthing out.
> Stuck in som extry goods
> Put the ship about.

To anyone that finds it in this blasted hole
Sam Slacum,
Master Mariner. Thresler 19—

Then as an after thought:

"Keep up your spirits."

The date was a year after the date on the post. The cache had not been visited evidently since then. For three years it had lain here, and for three years, evidently, only one ship had put in. This dismal thought took all the pleasure away from the find, she sat down on the rocks forming the mound and holding the paper in her fingers gave way for a moment to a depression that came against her like a black, surging sea. Then she remembered that the cross had been only visible from one point, that vessels might have been here and not have seen it, that men might even have landed and found it without leaving the fact behind them, after the manner of the writer of this paper.

And then, suddenly, and as if from the sky came the thought of Providence, the feeling that she had been led along the beach to find the wood and to find this. The remembrance of how she had been saved from the *Gaston de Paris* rose up in her mind also—saved almost by a miracle.

To a person torn from civilization and flung into the arms of Nature the most terrible thing is the sense of the amorphous, the feeling that there is no structure in this world where houses are not and laws are not and streets are not, no power to intervene between oneself and injury, no thread to cling to. The idea of a Providence to such a person is like brandy.

The girl remembered the words she had spoken that morning to her companions when she said that one must not think here but work. There was no use in thinking of the past or the future, of ships coming or not, they had been taken care of so far and the feeling came to her that this would be so to the end.

She rose up, put the paper back in the box and the box in her pocket, then she turned to the cache.

She walked round the mound to a spot where the covering rocks had fallen away a bit and going down on her knees began pulling them apart and carrying them off one by one, dumping them a few yards away. Her rings hindered her and taking them off she put them in the tobacco box and the box in her pocket. Under the rocks lay a covering of sand, she fetched the arm of the cross and scraping away at the sand came upon something hard, it was the end of a barrel. Then she stood up, flushed with her work and satisfied.

The stores were there, whatever they might be, and with the help of the two men they would easily be uncovered. The question whether they would be of any use after all the years they had lain there recurred to her, but she put it aside. They would soon see.

Then she started back for the caves taking the slat of wood with her as a trophy. As she went the recollection of the find followed her agreeably, she did not know which to congratulate herself most upon, the wood of the wreck or the cache. Then came the dismal thought of winter, begotten of the idea of fires. It was the middle of August. Winter lay ahead. If no ship came to take them off what would their life be like during the winter months? Imagine this place at Christmas, covered perhaps with snow! The gloom of this idea pursued her for a mile or more till all of a sudden she stopped and laughed aloud at her own stupidity. It was not autumn, it was spring. They were south of the line and summer lay before them, not winter. That gloomy ghost, fear of the Future, which spoils so many men's lives in Civilization, had tricked her and made her miserable and as she cast it from her and pursued her way she said to herself again: "I will not think, here the person who thinks and broods is lost."

When she reached the caves the men had not yet returned; leaving the slat of wood leaning against the cliff she came down to the boat and stood for a moment looking at the sea. The tide was far out now and coming in again, the sea had fallen to a gentle glassy swell and the treacherous wind had died away to a faint breeze. Out there where the waves were coming in and at the limit of the sands rocks were uncovered, shaggy, black rocks that seemed covered with fur. She came down to them and found that the fur was a coating of mussels. Here was another find. She began to pick them and then, running back to the cave for the baling tin, filled it to the brim, and placed it in the boat. Having done this she sat down with her back to the boat to rest and wait for the men.

They ought to have returned by this. The thought that some disaster had happened to them came to her and tried to creep into her mind, but she drove it out promptly, stamped on it and began to think of how they would cook the mussels. They would make a fire with the slat she had brought back, it was tarred and would burn finely, with that and some of the bottom boards of the boat, unless Bompard could be persuaded to go and cut some wood from the wreckage three miles away. Then she thought how fortunate it was that men smoked. La Touche had a Swedish match box nearly full of matches and Bompard had a tinder box, one of the sort that makes a spark by the striking of a wheel against a flint.

Then she yawned.

She had been in the open air since early dawn and it was now noon. She was not tired, but she was filled with a craving for something, yet she could not tell what this something was that she wanted and without which she felt somehow lost. Then she knew—it was a roof.

A person accustomed to live under a roof and suddenly condemned to live in the open suffers nothing for the first few hours. Then there gradually comes upon him a weariness and distress almost unimaginable to those who have not experienced it. He craves not only for a roof but for walls around him to protect him from the great open spaces that seem sucking away his individuality. A man living absolutely in the open without tent or cave or house wherein to concentrate himself would surely and without doubt either become mad or descend to the level of the beasts.

She came up the beach to the cave where she had slept, went into it, and sat down, her mind finding instant relief from the craving that had filled it. Her hands went up to her hair and began to arrange it as best they could. Had she been alone on the beach she would have taken the pins out and left it loose for the winds to comb and blow about, but the thought of the men prevented her. She did not like the idea of their seeing her going about with her hair down; after her experiences in the boat it seemed absurd to quibble over a thing like this and she tried to argue with herself without avail. It seemed to her that if she went about in *negligé* like that she would lower herself. How? There was nothing unwomanly in flowing hair, there was nothing indelicate. No, but women of her class never appeared before men in that fashion, she would lower herself socially.

A fool would have laughed at her, holding that amidst castaways there was no such thing as social position, and, though fools are not inevitably wrong in their opinions, he would have been wrong.

Though Bompard and La Touche had dropped the "mademoiselle" in addressing her, they treated her since landing with a certain respect which would have been wanting had she been a woman of their own class.

The class difference held and was a greater protection to her than anything else. In their eyes she was not a woman, but a lady, a fact that chilled familiarity, or worse, and, with the aid of her superior intelligence, gave her authority.

She felt this instinctively and determined that at no time and in no manner would she allow her position to degrade.

Then, having done what she could to her hair she took the rings from the tobacco box and put them on. She would have much preferred not to have worn them, they irritated her, but they were part of her insignia and she put them on.

As she was putting the tobacco box back in her pocket something looked in at her. It was a rabbit, a grey fat rabbit that had lopped right to the cave mouth; it sat up for a moment on its hind legs, looked in, and then lopped off without any hurry, as though a girl seated in a cave were an accustomed object and a human being something not to be afraid of.

This fearlessness of the rabbit would have started her on a long and dismal train of thought had she not checked herself in time and like the man in the haunted house who kept the fear of ghosts away by thinking of plum puddings, she started to work, re-folding the sail that had served her for a pillow the night before; then she took the oilskin coat out and shook it, and folding it, placed it by the left wall of the cave with the sou'wester on top of it. She was tidying her house.

Then she went into the men's cave and did a bit of tidying there, stacking the tins more neatly and putting the odds and ends together. The sight of the cotton waste gave her an idea and going down to the boat she emptied the mussels from the baling tin on to the sand, filled the tin with sea water and bathed her face and hands, drying them on the cotton. She had finished this operation and had got the mussels back in the tin when a shout caused her to turn.

It was the men, they were coming along the beach from the break in the cliffs. Bompard leading, La Touche lagging behind.

Bompard was carrying something under his arm, it was a Kerguelen cabbage. La Touche carried nothing.

XI

The Cache

When she lay down that night on the hard sand, with the sailcloth beneath her head, she could not sleep. The wretchedness of having to lie down fully dressed, of being unable to change her clothes, fell on her like a blight.

She lay fighting the problem. It was impossible to go on like this. One might live with little food, but to live always without undressing and changing one's things was impossible. This problem was insoluble, or seemed so. Then she found a half solution. She would discard her stockings and under garments, make a bundle of them and put them under the sailcloth, she would not wear them again, she would suffer from cold, no matter, anything was better than that feeling of being fully dressed always. The weather, besides, was fairly warm. She would learn to do without shoes as well as without stockings. She would have to go about without shoes or stockings. She thought of the men. Strangely enough the thought of going about without shoes or stockings seemed less repulsive to her than the thought of going about with her hair loose.

As she lay revolving this business in her mind the whale birds flitting about in the darkness outside suddenly ceased their crying and through the silence came a vague mysterious sound that deepened into a humming like the drone of a gigantic top; the humming became a roar, the roar of rain. Rain falling in solid sheets, coming across the land like a moving Niagara, now taking the beach and now the sea. Never had she heard such rain as this, falling in the black and utter darkness. The shelve of the beach saved the cave from being flooded and the beetling of the cliff kept it dry and within a couple of feet of the entrance but it could not keep out the rain smell, the raw smell of Kerguelen carried from inland, the smell of bog patches and new washed dolerite and bitter vegetation, keen, like the smell of the Stone Age. Then after a bit the first great onslaught slackened.

The girl raised herself on her elbow, then she rose and cast off the oilskin coat that had served for a blanket. She undressed in the darkness, made a bundle of her stockings and her Jaeger underclothes and placed them beneath the sailcloth, then removing the comb from her hair and letting it fall she came out into the blackness and stood in the torrential rain.

It beat on her head and shoulders and breast, it cascaded down her limbs, soothing as the hand of mesmerism, refreshing, delightful beyond words, then she came back into the cave and, finding the cotton waste, dried herself as well as she could, dried her hair and twisted it into a knot, put on her blouse, coat and skirt and covered herself with the oilskin.

She had solved the question of a bath and change of clothes, at least for the moment. The discomfort of the rough tweed of the skirt against her unprotected limbs, of the hard bed, of the sailcloth pillow with its vague smell of canvas and jute, all these were nothing to that other discomfort. These were physical, that was psychical.

She fell asleep and slept till long after dawn. When she came out the rain had ceased and through air fresh as though from the hand of Creation vast clouds were rolling away towards the islands over a blue-green sea.

They had made a fire on the night before and had cooked some of the mussels in the baling tin, the rest had been put by to cook for breakfast; hot food of any sort is a revelation if you have been condemned to live on cold stuff for anytime, but this morning there was to be nothing hot. The firewood, one of the bottom boards of the boat chopped up, had been left out in the rain. The sight of it, all soaked, made the girl forget her bare feet and her hair roughly tied up in a knot. The housekeeper that lives in every woman rose up in revolt, all the more so as the guilty ones tried to defend themselves.

"As for me," said La Touche, "I was listening to the rain, it drove everything else out of my head."

"That is so," said Bompard, "I thought every moment we would be flooded out. It was no time for a man to be thinking of firewood."

"Well, you will have no fire and nothing hot," said Cléo, "and those mussels will be wasted—they won't keep, but there's no use in saying anymore about it—only you must learn to think of things. It's not pleasant, I know, to have to look ahead but one has to do it. You see I am not wearing my boots and stockings, boots wear out and stockings wear out quicker, so I just looked ahead last night and said to myself— 'your stockings will soon be worn into holes, so you must begin now to learn to do without them.' It's not pleasant, but it has to be done. If that ship we ran into had looked ahead we would not have been wrecked."

　　　　　　　　HENRY DE VERE STACPOOLE

"That is true," said Bompard, anxious to get off the main subject. "If those chaps had eyes in their heads they wouldn't be feeding the fishes."

"It wasn't all their fault," put in La Touche. "If those chaps on the bridge hadn't put the engines on we wouldn't have rammed her as we did."

"Well," said Cléo, "there is no use in going back over things. We have to get breakfast and then go and open the cache."

She had told them of the cache overnight and, to her wonder, the thing had interested them, so this morning when they had finished their biscuits and beef she found not the slightest difficulty in making them start.

She put on her boots for the journey and then they reeled along the beach in the usual order, Cléo first, the two others following; the great skull made them halt and discuss it for a moment but the figure-head when they reached it held them entirely in its spell.

She could scarcely tear them away, they discussed it from every point of view, argued over it, pondered over it and were only brought to their senses by a hint that it would have to be chopped up for firewood.

Then, when they reached the cache, there was another long pause for discussion, the two sitting down to smoke whilst they talked it over.

It was not till she set to work pulling more stones away that they began to get busy; then when once started they laboured like negroes. The glimpse of the barrel end seemed to inflame them, but indeed they did not want even that, for the business they had set their hands to had all the fascination of treasure hunting mixed with the thrills of house-breaking. Here was "stuff," plunder of some sort, who could tell what?

An hour and a half of labour brought them sweating to the end of the business and the presiding gulls saw exposed to the light of day two big barrels, two long cases and an amount of canned meat and vegetables enough to stock a small shop, also a harpoon of the old type and two shovels placed by the long cases. Then after a rest of half an hour the barrels were sampled. One contained flour, the other blankets and mens' clothes, sweaters and coats and trousers. One of the long cases contained kitchen utensils and tin cups and plates, also knives and forks and spoons.

The other contained "comforts," tea and coffee and sugar in sealed tins, some rolls of tobacco, drugs and a few surgical instruments. All the equipment, in fact, necessary for an expedition of a dozen men for six months. Not a drop of liquor.

Perhaps that was why the girl was more overjoyed by the details of the find than the mariners.

Bompard openly expressed his mind.

"Not a bottle of wine or a drop of rum, swabs."

"Well, you've got some tobacco," said Cléo, "and there's tea and coffee and cups and saucers, and a teapot—no coffeepot—well one can make coffee in anything—" She was running over the stores in her mind, standing, reviewing them with no thought of anything else and her soul filled with a joy and satisfaction absolutely new.

Blankets! Tea! Coffee! and clothes—even mens' clothes if it came to the worst. One might have fancied her to have fixed definitely in her mind that she was to spend a very long time on the shores of Kerguelen and to have accepted the terrible prospect with equanimity. It was not so. She was living in the moment, so entirely in the moment that these things were tremendous and vivid and compared with them Art, Music, Religion, Ambition, and the gauds of Civilization were as nothing.

This power to live in the moment is the form of strength that brings men through battles and women through adversity. It fells cities and builds them. On Kerguelen it is salvation. For, here to think of the future, unless in terms of material necessities, to dream, to brood, means death or madness.

But Bompard and La Touche, resting themselves after their labours, were not living in the moment nor in the past nor in the present, they were living in that strange sad land called the Might-Have-Been. They might have been in the way to a jolly booze by now if that fool who provisioned the cache had not forgotten the drink. They were thankful for nothing. They had food, they had clothes, they had tobacco. They were glad enough of the blankets, but even the thought of the blankets could not relieve their depression.

They were not drunkards, but the cache had given them hopes of drinks. These hopes shattered they sat like discontented children who had been promised sweets and disappointed.

But this did not last long, the Hopeless is its own antidote and after half a pipe of tobacco their cheerfulness, such as it was, returned and they fell to discussing with the girl the best way of treating the stores.

Bompard, considering the difficulty of transporting the stuff to the caves, proposed that they should move their abode right up to the cache.

Cléo pointed out that there were no caves here, so, unless they moved the caves as well as their belongings, they would have nowhere to sleep in.

"I think the best thing we can do," said she, "is to take what we want and then cover up the rest till we want some more."

"Put the stuff under the rocks again?" asked Bompard.

"Yes."

"Mon Dieu!" said La Touche.

It was not what he said but the way he said it that angered the girl.

La Touche was a problem in her mind. She could understand Bompard but she could not quite understand La Touche. It seemed to her that he was one of those people who without much intelligence, yet, or perhaps because of that fact, make fine centres of rebellion. She could fancy him leading a mob to tear down something that vexed him, and everything seemed to vex him, at times.

But though she was not clear about La Touche she was quite clear about herself and she was determined to be his master. She felt instinctively that he was the leader of Bompard and that Bompard alone would have been a much better individual, in many respects.

"There is no use in saying 'Mon Dieu,'" said she, "the thing has to be done. The gulls and the rabbits will ruin everything if we leave things about. Come, Bompard."

Bompard rose up at the order and began to assist in sorting out the things they were to take back with them. Then La Touche, not to be out of the business and perhaps ashamed of himself, or of his position as an idler, joined in.

Had she given the order direct to him he might have revolted; she had conquered him for the moment none the less.

First they began to sort out the things to be kept for immediate use. A saucepan, three tin cups, three tin plates, knives and forks, the teapot and kettle, a canister of tea, sugar and salt. The canned stuff, including thirty cans of vegetables, Cléo left untouched. She determined to keep it in reserve and depend upon the cabbage plants, one of which Bompard had brought back yesterday.

Then came the question of the flour, that too must be kept in reserve and the opening they had made in the top of the barrel closed up properly. This operation took time and was conducted with a good deal of grumbling which fell on deaf ears. The thing was done and that was the main thing. Four blankets were taken from the other barrel and that too was closed. Then with the shovels the whole lot was sanded over and the rocks replaced, the girl helping in the work as well as directing.

When everything was finished they made three bundles, using the blankets as holdalls, and started back.

It was now noon and the breeze that had been blowing ever since dawn had died away, but great clouds were banking up over the islands, vast, solemn, leaden-coloured clouds rolling up from the far sea and piling one on the other like alps on alps.

They had nearly reached the caves when a roll of thunder like the ruffle of muffled drums came over the water, but they got under shelter before the rain began to fall, just a few heavy drops, at first, and then in a moment a cataract.

The islands vanished, the sea vanished to within a few hundred yards of the beach, the voices of the gulls and the breaking of the waves became merged and vague in the hiss of the sheeting rain.

"The chaps that left the truck in that cask forgot to shove in some oilskins," said La Touche as he undid his load.

Cléo had come into the men's cave to help to unpack. Half-way back she had taken her boots off. Owing to the absence of stockings her right heel had become chafed and she had taken them off determining not to wear them anymore. She was kneeling now, bare-footed, taking the things from Bompard's bundle and La Touche's remark made her look up. It was the tone rather than the words that irritated her. The recollection of an oilskin coat which she had used when fishing in Norway the year before rose in her mind. It had been put away for a long time and when taken out had been found all stuck up and quite ruined.

"You can't be much of a sailor," said she, "not to know that oilskin doesn't stand packing. The men who buried these things did. If they had known that you were so particular about rain they might have put in an umbrella."

Dead silence followed this thrust of the tongue which she instantly regretted, not because of hurting La Touche's feelings, but because she instantly felt that it had helped to widen the division between her and her mates. The extraordinary fact was that she, having assumed the responsibility of office, was, seemingly, held responsible by the others for all unpleasant happenings; she felt that the rain of Kerguelen was now, in a way, being laid at her door.

Then, again, she had singled out La Touche as a direct opponent.

She felt that he and she were already matching each other and there was likely to be a struggle between them for dominance.

Women have been gifted above men with an instinctive knowledge of character. She divined in La Touche a character weak yet capable of violence, incapable of leading yet jealous of being led, and especially of being led by a woman. That was the danger point.

However, there was no use in trying to say anything smooth and she went on with her work, helping to stow the things and, when that was finished, taking off two of the blankets to her own cave.

A fire was impossible owing to the rain so they dined off biscuits and canned stuff, cold.

Bompard and La Touche on this little expedition had discovered a water source only a quarter of a mile inland, a deep pond cut in the rocks and fed by the rains. Bompard referred to it as he ate.

"But as long as the boat holds together," said he, "we don't want to bother about water; she'll catch and hold all we want. I've heard tell it rains here months on end."

"When it's not blowing," said La Touche. Cléo said nothing. It came to her almost as a new impression that conversation as we know it was almost impossible with her companions. They had no outlook over anything but the material and they seemed to see nothing but the black side of things. She felt also that any attempt to rally them and cheer them would be dumbly resented and would only help to widen even more the division between her and them.

When the meal was finished she put the plates out in the rain to wash them. Then a bright idea came to her and getting the roll of wire she asked La Touche to shew her how to make rabbit snares.

La Touche took the roll of wire and held it in his hands for a moment.

"This is all very well," said he, "but where is your wire cutters?"

They had nothing to cut the wire with, and he seemed to look on the fact as a triumph of his own cleverness over Cléo's, till Bompard intervened and shewed how, by knotting the wire and pulling hard, a break might be made. This accomplished, and three lengths of wire having been procured, the surly one proceeded to make a snare and to demonstrate how it might be set.

At the end of the business the girl regretted that she had ever started it. She had put herself under the tuition of La Touche and allowed the intimacy of master and pupil, allowed even in this slight way that he was her superior.

A yelling wind from the mountains arose that afternoon and drove the rain away across the islands. It held for half an hour and then of a sudden ceased and a howling wind from the islands rose and drove the rain back again towards the mountains.

The sea suddenly seemed to go mad, with cross currents meeting. Waves seemed fighting waves and the gulls seemed filled with the general torment, clanging and blowing about hither and thither like leaves in autumn.

Cléo went to her cave and wrapping herself in one of the blankets, with the other folded double to lie upon, took her place upon the floor with her head on the sailcloth.

It was her first really bad moment. Her first moment of real depression. The rain and the fact that their position as regarded food was secure, so that there was nothing to fight against at the moment, conspired to overthrow her.

Hitherto she had fought bravely and the struggle had kept her up; the sudden easing of the situation had brought new forces against her. Time suddenly appeared before her eyes asking: "How are you to kill me? You can't, you have no weapons. Would you like a book? Would you like embroidery work to do, companions to talk with, music to listen to? Fate, under the name of civilization, gave you all these and more, they have been taken from you and now you see me as I am, the great terror."

She fought this Bogey by thinking of La Touche. She had raised La Touche against herself. She knew that something in herself had risen against La Touche.

She felt that his respect for a woman of the higher classes was, as regarded herself, wearing thin, owing to propinquity. That he resented being "bossed" by a woman, that her superior quickness of mind and energy vexed him and that one day he would try to master her. He was of the type that is too mean to rule, yet hates to be ruled. There was also the jealousy of the male at the superiority of the female. She was physically weaker than he, a fact that means little in civilized life where power is in the hands of Order, but which means everything in primitive life. And they were steadily drifting to the primitive.

These thoughts, troublesome enough, were still excellent in their way. They gave her occupation for her mind.

Then she fell asleep, awaking towards evening to find Bompard at the cave mouth telling her that supper was ready.

HENRY DE VERE STACPOOLE

XII

The Quarrel

Next morning broke fine. She was awakened by voices quarrelling and came out to find a breezy and absolutely cloudless day, with the sea running smooth and the sunlight on the far islands.

The two men, who had fallen out over some trifle, were wrangling like fish-women, Bompard having the worst of it, as his ineffectual southern oaths were no match for the language of the other.

The girl stood looking at La Touche, but he seemed not to mind in the least.

Then she turned away and walked down to the boat.

She heard Bompard say: "There, you have sent her off, talking like that," and what La Touche replied she could not hear, but she guessed it was something not complimentary to Bompard or herself.

The boat was half full of rain-water. She rinsed her hands in it, then, standing with the warm sun upon her, she almost forgot the men, looking at the purple islands and the gulls like new minted gold and the great arch of the bay lined out with a thread of creamy foam.

After a while, turning round, she saw that Bompard was lighting a fire with the remains of the wood and, coming up, she helped in the business.

He had arranged the little fire between pieces of rock so as to make a stand for the kettle, and La Touche was opening the hermetically sealed canister of tea with his knife; neither man was speaking and the meal passed off almost in silence.

She felt that any moment the quarrel might break out again and her instinct was to get away from them.

She had left the fisherman's knife and belt in her cave; she went to the cave and strapped the belt around her waist. The boat hook was lying on the sand; she picked it up and, carrying it, walked away down the beach in the direction of the cache.

The boat hook was a weapon of sorts and it was better out of the men's way; the knife was different. It had come to her that in this place it was better to be armed and she determined always to wear it.

But no sounds of quarrelling followed her, only the quarrelling of the gulls, and half a mile away, looking back, she saw that the men had separated. La Touche was standing by the boat and Bompard was walking towards the Lizard point. She sat down to rest for a moment and she watched the figure of Bompard. It grew smaller and smaller till it reached the point, then it vanished over the rocks.

She saw La Touche walk away towards the caves; he disappeared, and the beach, now destitute of life, lay sung to by the sea and flown over by the gulls. Nothing speaking of man lay there but the boat that looked like a toy cast there by a child. It held her eyes, focussed her thoughts, and became the centre of a sudden longing, a desire soul searching as the desire for water—the desire for civilization, for the things and people that she knew.

Her companions had become horrible to her. To go on living with them seemed appalling. The rocks, the sea, the gulls, even the rain, all these fitted with her mind—they seemed in some way familiar, but with the men she had nothing in common.

It is worse to be wrecked on a social state than on a desert shore. She was wrecked on both.

She recognised surely that at the rate things were going she would soon, so far from being above her companions, be below them on account of her weakness. She recognised that superiority of mind would count little after a while with these minds, incapable of distinguishing grades, or values, beyond money value and the distinction of master from man, and that sex so far from being a protection would be a danger.

Her brave mind allowed itself to be borne along for a while on these currents of thought, then it reacted against them, repeating again the old formula that to think, here, on other things than the moment and the material was to die or go distraught.

She got up and shifted her position, sitting with her back towards the boat.

She could see the penguins, now, drilling beneath the cliff and beyond the penguins the figure-head of the ship and beyond that the fuming beach with its snow storm of gulls. She was soon to see something that many would travel a thousand miles to witness, but unconscious of what was coming she sat watching the penguins, then with the boat hook point she began scratching figures on the sand, but with difficulty, on account of the length of the staff.

Sitting like this her eyes were suddenly attracted seaward to a point in the water beyond the line of the figure-head. Things were moving out there, moving rapidly and drawing in-shore and now, riding an incoming wave, like a half submerged canoe, she saw a dark elongated form. It came shooting through the foam just like a beaching canoe and as it dragged itself up the sand a sound like the far off roar of a lion came echoing along the cliffs.

She knew at once what it was, a sea elephant. Prince Selm had described them and how they came ashore at Kerguelen to breed, journeying there through thousands of miles of ocean and arriving in hundreds and thousands at different points of the coast.

This was the first of the great herd and, as she watched, more were coming, breasting the waves and breaking from the foam and coming up the beach like vast, rapidly-moving slugs.

The sight held her fascinated. Every newcomer saluted the land with a roar. They were the males; the females of the herd, still far out at sea beyond the islands, would not land to give birth to their young for another fortnight.

She watched till perhaps two hundred had beached, then the invasion ceased; there was no more roaring, and over the army of invaders, lumping along hither and thither on the flat rocks, the sea-gulls flew and screamed in anger or in welcome, who could say?

Prince Selm had spoken of how the sea elephants fought together on landing. He was wrong. The great, far-distant brutes instead of fighting seemed resting and sunning themselves and the girl, rising up, came along in their direction. She had forgotten Bompard and La Touche.

She reached the river which was spating from the recent rains, but great flat-topped rocks made it always possible to cross; she crossed it.

The sea elephants were close to her now and seemed not in the least disturbed by her presence, they lay here and there, vast brutes, twenty feet in height, weighing tons, raising themselves occasionally on their flippers and then sinking back to rest with a sigh of contentment.

She measured them with her eye, noted the short trunks that seemed so useless, the tusks, the old scar marks got in battle and the splendour of their strength and mass and muscle. Like the land elephants there was something about them terrible yet benign.

She drew closer. As regarded animals of any good sort she had the fearlessness of a child, the instinct that would have been terrified by a reptile or anything truly ferocious however masked by fur or feather. These things she felt to be absolutely harmless, as regarded herself, and they were a million years closer to her than the penguins.

The penguins had amused her, but for all their quaintness and politeness they seemed as far apart from her as mechanical toys. Her heart had not gone out to them with that love of living things which lies in the heart of children, of women and most men.

She drew closer still. The great brutes were now watching her steadfastly, but seemingly without fear. She had left the boat hook behind a mile away, dropping it because of its weight, and with the exception of the knife in her belt she was unarmed. Perhaps they knew this. Vague in their brains must have lain memories of great hurts when they were the hunted and men the hunters; but this vision evidently stored up no antagonistic feelings. Possibly they knew her sex and possibly the instinct which never failed them told them that she was friendly.

Less than ten yards away from the nearest bull she sat down on a piece of rock, and no sooner had she taken her seat than they seemed immensely closer and her own position one of absolute helplessness. With a sudden rush, moving with that swiftness with which she had seen them moving on first landing, the bull could have reached her, but the bull did not move, his lordship from the sea, filled with the absolute and complete contentment of the male at rest, moved only his trunk, he seemed sniffing her and the momentary fear that had seized her passed utterly away.

She could sniff him too. Just as cows fill the air with the fragrance of milk the herd filled the place with the scent of fish and fur and a tang of deep sea like the smell of beach, only sharper and fresher.

Then, just as people talk to horses and dogs, leaning forward a bit she began to talk to him.

The effect of the sweet soothing voice was magical, and for a moment not in the least soothing. The near bulls moved, evidently deeply disturbed in their minds. The majority, including the biggest and nearest bull, turned half away as if to get off, then turned again as if to renew their astonishment.

The girl laughed, the timidity of this vast force seemed to her less timidity than masculine awkwardness, as though a number of heavy old gentlemen, taking their ease in their club, were suddenly put to confusion and flight by a female charmer appearing before them.

XIII

WHERE IS BOMPARD?

When they had re-settled themselves she rose to go, nodded to them and turned away towards the river. Then she looked back. The big bull was following her and the rest of the herd were moving slightly in the same direction. The bull paused when she turned, then, when she went on, he continued following her, lazily and as if drawn by some gentle magnetic attraction.

Across the river she turned and waved her hand to them. Then she went on.

In some extraordinary way the creatures had made the place less lonely and the wonder of them pursued her as she walked, keeping to the sand patches where the rocks were and then striking along the great levels of pure sand.

Her feet did not hurt her and she was beginning to recognise that touch with the world which comes to those who walk without boots, something that humanity has all but forgotten, all but ceased to remember.

As she drew near the caves she looked for the men, but the beach was deserted. Then, looking into the men's cave, she saw La Touche lying on his back asleep, his pipe beside him and his arm flung across his eyes.

Where was Bompard?

He ought to have been back by this, and as she turned and looked up and down the beach a vague uneasiness came upon her.

It was as if for the first time she had recognized the value of Bompard in their small society. Bompard with his age and heaviness and patent honesty, despite his stupidity, was a presence not to be despised.

If La Touche had been another man she might have awakened him to make enquiries. As it was, she preferred to let him lie.

Bompard she had last seen crossing the rocks of the Lizard point. It was there that she must look for him.

She went to the cave where she had left her boots and put them on for the climb. When she reached the point she found the work easier than she had suspected. The rocks were not strewn at random, they were in reality breaks off and tables of the basalt; the whole point was like a great lizard that, creeping stealthily towards the sea, had been stricken into rock.

She climbed, and in five minutes was on the highest point with a new view of the coast before her. It was like looking at Ferocity. Here the rocks were broken and tumbled about, indeed, rocks, huge and spired like churches, cliffs black and polished with the washing of the waves, monoliths standing out in the blue-green water and all ringing and singing to the chime of the sea. Inland, cañons of night and shoulders of dolerite and plains where nothing grew leading to great level bastions, fortifications that seemed built by rule and plumb line, with the markings of the basalt visible through the clear air. Basalt has that terrible peculiarity. It seems the work of a hand, it makes castles and fortifications whose ruled markings bear the inevitable suggestions of masonry.

And across all that not a sign of life save the wings of the tireless birds, teal and duck, cormorants, and beyond the seaward rocks the great sea geese fishing and the guillemots flighting and the white tern darting like dragon-flies.

Where was Bompard?

Had he, by any chance, come back and taken someother road off the beach? There was only one way: the break in the cliffs, beyond the caves. She thought it highly improbable that he would have come back only to leave the beach by another way, the descent from where she stood and towards the bed country was quite easy, alluringly easy. No, he would have gone on.

She sat down to rest and watch.

At any moment he might appear in the distance. From where she sat the sea lay straight before her and the far off islands, to the left the rock strewn coast, to the right the great curving beach.

Behind her the country stormed away, stern, grey-grim and treeless, to the foothills whose misty mauve lay stretched before the mountains.

Every now and then she would turn towards the left searching the country and cliffs with her eyes, but no form appeared.

She remembered now that he had talked about sea birds' eggs and how to get them. Might he have gone hunting for eggs over those cliffs and fallen?

She remembered also when the two men had come back from their expedition inland they had brought an alarming story of a bog like a quick sand. La Touche had blundered into it and he would have gone down only for his companion. They had also said something about pot holes like shafts in the basalt. She turned her mind away from these thoughts and passing her fingers through her hair removed the comb which held it in a rough knot, shaking it free to the sun and wind. She combed it with her fingers and rearranged it and then looked again— nothing.

It came to her suddenly that though she were to sit there forever the vigil would be useless, that Bompard had gone—never to return.

She reasoned with this feeling, and reason only increased her fears. It was now noon, Bompard was not the man to go on a long expedition by himself; he was too inactive and easy-going. No, something had happened to him and he might at that moment be lying dead at the foot of some cliff or he might have broken a leg and be lying at the foot of some rock unable to move.

She rose up and came swiftly down to the beach. Reaching the caves she found La Touche opening a tin. It was dinner-time.

"What has become of Bompard?" she asked. "Have you seen him since he went off this morning over those rocks?"

"Bompard," replied the other, "Mon Dieu! How do I know? No, I have not seen him, he is big enough to take care of himself."

"That may be," she replied, "but accidents happen no matter how big a man may be. He has not returned—"

"So it would seem," said La Touche, who had now got the tin open and was turning the contents on to a plate. "But he will return when he remembers that it is dinner-time."

Her lips were dry with anger, there was a contained insolence in the manner and voice of the other that roused her as much as his callousness. His mind seemed as cold as his pale blue eyes. All her mixed feelings towards him focussed suddenly into a point—she loathed him; but she held herself in.

"If he has not returned when we have finished dinner," said she, "we will have to look for him." She took a plate and some of the beef he had turned from the tin and with a couple of biscuits drew off and taking her place outside in the sun began her wretched meal. A rabbit that had run out on the sands sat up and looked at her as she ate, then it ran off and as she followed it with her eyes she contrasted the little friendly form with the form of La Touche, the dark innocent eyes with those eyes of washed-out blue, without depth, or, perhaps, veiling depth.

When she had finished eating she put the plate by her side and sat waiting for La Touche to make a movement.

Bompard that morning had left his tinder box behind him in the cave, she heard the strike of flint on steel. La Touche was lighting his pipe. She waited ten minutes or more, then she came to the cave mouth.

"Are you not coming to look for Bompard?" asked she.

"I'll go when I choose," said he, "I don't want orders."

"I gave you no orders," she replied, "I asked you, are you not coming to look for Bompard who may be in difficulties, or lying perhaps with a broken limb—and you sit there smoking your pipe. But I give you orders now; get up and come and help to look for him. Get up at once."

He sprang to his feet and came right out. It seemed to her that she had never seen him before. This was the real La Touche.

"One word more from you," he shouted, "and I'll show you who's master. You! Talk to me, would you! A—woman more trouble than you're worth. Off with you, get down the beach—clear!"

He took a step forward with his right fist ready to strike, open-handed. Then he drew back. She had whipped the knife from its sheath.

The boat hook, which she had brought back with her, was propped against the cliff behind her and out of his reach, he had no weapon.

She did not add a word to the threat of the knife. He stood like a fool, unable to sustain her gaze, venomous, yet held, as a snake is held by a man's grip.

"Now," she said, "get on. Go search for your companion and if you dare to speak to me again like that I will make you repent it. You thought I was weak being a woman and alone. You were going to strike. Coward!—Get on, go and search for your companion."

He turned suddenly and walked off towards the Lizard rocks. "I'll go where I choose," said he.

It was a lame and impotent end of his rebellion, but she held no delusions. This was only the beginning—if Bompard did not return.

She put the knife in its sheath and then she put the boat hook away, hiding it behind the sailcloth in her cave, then she went into the men's cave. La Touche's clasp knife lay there on the sand, it was not much of a weapon but she took it. She examined the dinner knives again. They were almost useless as weapons. Then she came out. La Touche had disappeared beyond the rocks and she came to the boat. There was nothing here in the way of a weapon that he might use, unless the oars. They were heavy, but he was strong. She determined to leave nothing to chance and, carrying the oars down the beach to the break in the cliffs, she hid them amongst some scrub bushes. Then she remembered the axe, sought for it and hid it.

Then she came back and sat down to reconsider matters.

The position was as bad as could be.

As bad as La Touche. Once let this man get the upper hand and she was lost. She would be his slave and worse. She had measured him finely. Instinct, never at fault, told her that to pull down anything above him would be meat and drink to La Touche's true nature and that his hatred of her superiority was deepened by the fact that she was a woman.

Were she weak he would beat her and make her cook for him, trample on her, make her his woman to fetch and carry, and, if Bompard did not come back, she was here alone with him and would have to fight this thing out.

Well, she could not fight it by brooding over it, and she was not helping to look for Bompard.

She drew the knife from its sheath and held the eight inches of razor sharp steel balanced in her hand for a moment as though admiring it. Then she replaced it in the sheath and started towards the Lizard Point.

XIV

The Death Traps

From the highest shoulder of the point she could see La Touche clambering over the seaward rocks.

He seemed more in search of shells and seaweed than of Bompard. Then, climbing down, she reached the lower ground and struck off inland. If she did not succeed in finding Bompard she would at least succeed in avoiding La Touche.

Right from the Lizard Point the plain stretched to higher ground which marked the beginning of the sea cliffs, great rocks strewed the way and the ground was torn by the beds of small water courses, depressions that would suddenly become little rivers in the deluging rains; stunted bushes huddled as if for shelter at the rock bases and the voice of the sea came here, broken and mixing with the whisper of the bushes to the wind.

This place had once been a glacier bed, rounded boulders standing in pools of water told that.

A gull flying in from the sea and carrying a fish in its beak drew her attention; it was being pursued by a larger gull. They were both of the Burgomaster type, but the fish carrier was noticeable on account of the intense blackness of its tail plumage.

As they passed the fish dropped, fell on a patch of yellow ground just in front of the girl, sank, and vanished.

She stopped dead and drew back with a chill at her heart. Then she picked up a stone and cast it on the patch of ground. It vanished even more swiftly than the fish.

It was one of the bogs the men had spoken of. They had described the treacherous ground as white, this was yellowish and not very noticeable, it was also death and another dozen steps would have led her into it.

She advanced cautiously, reached the border line and kneeling down pushed her hand into the yellow mud. It was like pushing it into a cold slimy mouth. She could scarcely draw it out again, when she did the mud was clinging to her hand like a yellow glove.

She came back to one of the rock ponds and washed her hand, it was like trying to get rid of treacle and, as she washed, she tried to fancy what would have happened but for the gull, tried to picture herself being slowly pulled down into that cold darkness and entombed there forever.

Then, skirting the place of danger, she went on, cautiously, examining carefully the ground before her. She had not gone ten yards when it seemed to her that a patch right in front of her was ever so slightly darker and moister looking than the ground she was treading.

She picked up a stone and cast it on the patch. It vanished. Then she knew the feeling of the man who finds himself ambuscaded.

This place was a death trap, or, rather, a series of death traps, there might be pits lying in wait for her quite unnoticeable. She turned and began to retrace her steps, so shaken that she would not trust even the ground that she had already covered but kept testing it by casting stones before her.

From a little distance an observer might have fancied her engaged in some new sort of game.

Near the safety of the Lizard rocks her eyes, closely scanning the ground before her, caught sight of something. It was a half-burned match. No one else but Bompard could have dropped that match. He had started without his tinder-box, had evidently found that match in his pocket, lit his pipe and walked on. There was only one direction in which he would have walked unless he had struck inland, which was improbable. He would have made as she had made to cross to the higher ground.

Even if he had walked inland he would not have escaped, for, casting her eyes in that direction she could see yellow patches spreading between the rocks.

She knew now what had become of Bompard, and with lips dry as pumice stone she began to climb till she reached the point where she had sat that morning. If the mud had taken Bompard, had he cried out? If so, La Touche would have heard his cries, for the caves were not so far from the Lizard rocks.

La Touche was nowhere to be seen, but she had no fear about him, or only the fear that he would come back. Bompard was gone. Bompard was dead, she knew it as though she had seen him engulfed, and she was here alone, in this place, with La Touche.

She put her hand to her side automatically to make sure that the knife was there. Then she sat with her eyes fixed on the distant islands, haze-purple in the light of the westering sun.

The thought of the boat on the beach came to her with the idea that she might launch it and escape, make for the islands and put all that sea between herself and the man she hated. But she could not launch the boat single-handed and, if she could, it would have been impossible to work it single-handed with those big oars.

She could see the boat from where she sat and the line of the beach leading away past the seal-nursery and the sea elephant strand to the rocks that formed the north-eastern horn of the bay. In stormy weather those rocks would be invisible in the smoke of the breakers, today they were clearly defined. She could see the great seals as they moved slowly hither and thither and the ship's figure-head as it stood to this side of them and, like a pin point of white the great white skull on the sands, a desolate scene, but almost benign when compared to the savagery of rocks and cliffs visible on her other side and that sinister plain, where the death traps were set and waiting with the patience of malignity for what might come to feed them.

She had fought the human failing that makes men brood and trouble about the future, a failing that is mostly born of houses and artificial life; already the struggle against it was less. She was coming more and more under that which has dominion over all things that live in the open and have to fight for life—the moment. If she had examined her own mind she would have found that the death of Bompard, of which she felt certain, affected her far less than it would have done some days ago, that her desire to escape to the islands was caused by the hatred of La Touche more than by fear of the future with him.

She would have found that her capacity for hatred had increased and also her dangerous qualities, and she would have found all this because God had so ordered life that it is adaptable, making the defensive and offensive qualities of the being capable of increase or decrease in answer to environment or need.

She came back to the beach. It wanted, still, a couple of hours of sun-down. There was no sign yet of La Touche, but, just as she knew in her heart that Bompard was dead she knew that La Touche was all right. He had been keeping to the rocks by the sea, leaving that aside; she knew that he would come back. He was of the sort that remains unscathed when the better man is taken.

She had one dread; that La Touche might get the knife from her, throw it away, and be master by his superior strength.

She had his clasp knife in her pocket, but it was a thing of little

HENRY DE VERE STACPOOLE

account in a struggle. Well, she must be on her guard. Then came the thought: "But how can I be on my guard when I am asleep?"

Nothing would be easier, if he were really in earnest, than for him to creep upon her whilst she slept, and disarm her.

She tried to dismiss this idea. La Touche was not crafty enough for that and, besides, would he go to the lengths of a physical struggle? He had been on the point of hitting her, it was true, but that was in a moment of excitement. Was she not painting him in too desperate colours?

Argue as she would on the question, reason, instinctive reason, always came back with the same answer: "Be on your guard, that knife is the only barrier between you and heaven knows what. Without it you would be at the mercy of a superior force. La Touche is no melodramatic villain; he is, what is perhaps worse for you, a creature of low instincts, stronger than you. Beware of being at his mercy."

With her mind filled by these thoughts she set to work getting supper ready. La Touche had taken the tinder box with him, so a fire was out of the question and she contented herself by laying out the beef that had served for dinner, and some biscuits.

Then she saw that she had only laid two plates. Working half-unconsciously she had ruled Bompard out. She looked at the things lying there on the sand, then she turned away from them. La Touche had crossed the rocks and was coming along the beach. He was trailing a long ribband of seaweed he had picked up and as he drew closer she saw that he had left his ill-humor behind him.

"There was no sight of Bompard," said he, "he has not come back, then?"

"Bompard will not come back," replied the girl, "we will never see him again."

Then she told of the death traps beyond the rocks and of the match.

La Touche listened, standing, and still holding the ribband of seaweed in his fingers.

She could see that he believed what she said and yet his words gave the lie to what was in his face.

"Oh, Bompard will come back all right," said he. "He's not such a fool as to get into any of those bogs; he's sulking, that's all."

He shaded his eyes, looking back towards the rocks as though on the chance of seeing the missing one; then he sat down before his plate and helped himself to food and the girl, loathing him and the food as well, sat down and made a pretence of eating.

She noticed that he was cheerful, for a wonder. He ate with good appetite and shewed in his movements and manner and voice when he spoke a restrained vivacity new to him.

His blondness, the washed-out blue of his eyes, his features, his voice, she considered all these anew as she sat opposite to him. It seemed to her that anything truly manly about him had come from the sea; that essentially he was a product of Mont Martre or the Banlieu of old Paris. She loathed him now as only a woman can loathe a man and, woman-like, her loathing focussed itself upon his blondness and the colour of his eyes.

Then, when she had done with the pretence of eating she rose up and, leaving him to remove the things, walked down to the water's edge and along towards the break in the cliffs.

The tide was nearly out and the sea scarcely broke on the rocks; she had never seen it calmer nor the islands closer. They seemed to have drawn in shore during the last half hour and as she looked she saw a great flock of gulls coming landward, and, as she turned to watch them, she noticed the far-off mountain tops visible through the cliff break. They were fuming. One might have fancied that fires had been lit all along their tops and round the highest peak a turban of cloud was winding itself, coil on coil.

Then as she stood watching, and from away over, there came a rumble, deep and cavernous, as if a gargantuan dray were being driven over subterranean roads. It died out in echoes amongst the foothills and the silence returned broken only by the wash of the sea on the beach.

She turned towards the sea. It had altered suddenly in colour and from away beyond the islands the wind was coming. She could see it, raking the sea like a comb. Then it struck the beach and yelled away up the break in the cliffs like a hunter in a hurry to get to the wild work going on amidst the hills.

She turned back towards the caves.

La Touche had left the tin plates lying on the sand and the wind, which seemed to possess a hundred fingers, was chasing them about. He was trying to recapture them and as he brought them back he laughed. It was the first time she had seen him laugh. Then as he stowed them away he shewed a disposition towards intimacy and talkativeness.

"That's what the winds are in this place," said he, "no wonder ships steer clear of it."

"I'm not thinking of the wind," said she, "I'm thinking of Bompard."

"Oh, Bompard will come back all right," said he, "the grub's here and that will bring him. Bompard will come back all right."

"No," said she, "he will never come back and you know it."

She turned away from him. Dusk was now falling and as she entered her cave the wind from the sea suddenly fell dead. Almost immediately it began to blow again, but now from the land and as though this land wind were spreading a pall over the sky darkness fell suddenly and with the darkness she could hear the rain coming with the sound she had heard once before like the murmuring of a great top spun by a giant.

Then the rain burst on the beach with a roar through which came the hiss of the rain-swept sea.

The sound was almost welcome. As she lay in the darkness it seemed like a protecting wall between herself and La Touche. La Touche's ill-temper would have disturbed her less than his cheerfulness and amiability, born so suddenly and from no apparent reasons. She had determined not to sleep and she had lain down fully dressed; even to the oilskin coat and with her boots on; tomorrow she would go off and hide amongst the bushes beyond the cliff break and get some sleep, but tonight she would not close her eyes; so she told herself.

She had taken the knife from its sheath and placed it beside her, her hand rested on it. An hour passed, and now, as she lay listening to the pouring of the rain her fingers felt the pattern of the hilt. The hilt was striated cross-ways to give a better grip, and as her fingers wandered up and down the strictions the cross bars of a ladder were suggested to her. The steady pouring of the rain seemed to work on this idea and make it more real. Then she was climbing a ladder set against the cliffs. La Touche was holding it at the foot and Bompard was waiting for her at the cliff top. He helped her up and then the dream changed to something else, and to something else, till she woke suddenly to the recognition that she had been asleep for a long time and that fear, deadly fear, was clutching her by the throat.

She sat up, leaning on her elbow. The rain was still falling, though the sound of it was much less, and the blackness was so intense that it seemed moulded round her. She felt for the knife and found it. Then she lay down again, listening.

The tide was coming in and she recognised, and not for the first time, a curious singing, chanting echo that always accompanied the waves of the incoming tide.

Fear is reasonless, it is also Protean, and this sea voice coming through the night turned the fear of La Touche to the fear of Bompard. What if he were to return, cold and wet, from that terrible grave-yard beyond the rocks?

XV

The Stroke

As she lay, listening, through the black darkness and the singing of the sea came a faint sound as of something dragging itself along the sand at the cave entrance. She clutched the knife and sat up. A waft of wind brought with it a tang of stale tobacco and rain-wet clothes. It was La Touche.

She drew up her feet and sat crouched against the sailcloth, the knife half-held in her lap, her fingers nerveless, her mind paralysed with the knowledge that now, immediately, she would *have* to fight, that the Beast was all but upon her. She knew.

She could hear him breathing now and the faint sound of his hands feeling gently over the floor of the cave. He was searching for her, the fume of him filled the place, he was almost in touch with her, yet still she sat helpless as a little child, paralysed in the blackness, as a bird before a crawling cat. Yet her right hand as though endowed with a volition of its own was tightening its grasp upon the hilt of the knife.

She had no longer reasoning power. Reasoning power and energy seemed now in the possession of the knife.

Then something touched her left boot and at the touch her hand struck out into the darkness, blindly and furiously, driving the knife home to the hilt in something that fell with a choking sound across her feet. She forced her feet from the thing that had suddenly fallen on them, rose, sprang across it and passed through the cave entrance with the surety of a person moving in broad daylight.

Then the pouring rain on her face brought her to her full senses and recognition of what had happened.

The knife was still in her hand and her hand was sticky and damp.

She said to herself: "That is his blood." The thought that perhaps she had killed him did not occur to her. The fear of him was still so intense, that it made him alive, alive somewhere in the surrounding darkness, and waiting to seize her. Then she began to steal off towards the sound of the sea. Twice as she went she stopped and turned, ready to strike again, then when the water was washing round her feet she came up the beach a few paces and crouched down.

The sea was at her back and the haunting dread of being followed vanished.

It was now that she asked herself the question: "Have I killed him?" Meaning:—"Have I freed myself of him,"—hoping this was so.

The terror behind her having vanished she was now brave. It seemed to her that the sound of the sea had become sharper; then she realized that the sound of the rain had ceased. Her mind seemed working in a dual manner and she had not fully recognized the cessation of the rain till the sound of the sea clinched the fact.

Through the clear night now came the melancholy crying of the whale birds, and through the broken clouds a ray of the moon shewed a faint light in which the cliffs began to stand out.

The incoming tide washed round her so that she had to move, it seemed determined to drive her up to the caves. She could see now the whole beach desolate of life and before her, vaguely sketched in the cliff wall, the cave openings.

She came along the sea edge till she reached the break in the cliffs, then, looking behind her again to make sure, she took refuge in the bushes.

For the last few yards before reaching them she seemed wading through tides of nothingness. In the shelter of the bushes she forgot everything.

HENRY DE VERE STACPOOLE

XVI

Alone

S he was awakened by the light of day. Kerguelen had cleared its face of clouds and the new risen sun was on sea and mountains and land.

A whole family of rabbits were disporting themselves close to her in a clear space between the bushes and as she sat up they darted off, a glimpse of their cotton white tails shewing for a moment in the sun.

She was stiff from the damp, her clothes were wet despite the oilskin coat which she had left open, and her throat was sore, every bone ached as though she had been beaten. Her soul felt sick. It was as though the crawling beast of the night before had crawled over it like a slug, poisoning it. The knife lay beside her; she picked it up and looked at it; there were red traces upon the hilt and the lines in the palm of her right hand were red. She rubbed it clean with the damp leaves of the bushes, then she stood up, shaking and weak, heedless of everything but the friendly touch of the sun. Her fear was gone, but the effect of it remained in a sense of bruising and injury.

Out on the beach there was nothing, nothing but the breaking sea and the flying gulls and lines of long legged gulls stalking or standing on the sands, the 'get-away—get-away' of the kittiwakes came across the water and the barking of brent geese from beyond the rocks of the Lizard Point. The boat lay there on its side, everything was the same.

She drew towards the caves. Nothing stirred there. Then she halted and, changing her course, came right down to the water's edge. From here she could see the three cave mouths dark cut in the cliff. She watched them for a moment as though expecting something to appear, then she came up towards them, walking more cautiously as she drew near, just as she had walked on the plain where the death traps were.

The light shone into the cave where she had slept. She saw a naked foot with toes dug into the sand and beyond the foot a form lying on its side.

Then she drew back with a cry; something was moving there. A rabbit dashed out of the cave and scuttered away along the cliff base. Then she knew.

La Touche was dead, he would never crawl again. She had killed him. She cast the knife on the sand and wiped the palm of her hand on her dress half unconsciously, gazing at the foot.

The terror of him had burned away anything in her mind that might have fed remorse. She had not killed him consciously. Searching her memory she could vaguely recollect having struck out against something appalling in the darkness. Now she knew and guessed all, and she could have hated him only that death kills hatred.

She came to the mouth of the men's cave and sat down in the sun, the soreness of her throat, the weariness of her very bones, the feel of her horrible wet clothes, all these filled her with a craving for the sun and its warmth and light, fierce as the craving for drink. She spread out her hands to it, then, with shaking fingers she began to take off her clothes. They clung to her like evil things. Had this been a day of pouring rain she might just have lain down and died.

Without getting up, and leaning on her elbow, she spread out the skirt and coat and other things on the sand beside her, then she stretched her aching limbs to the warmth.

The wind had fallen to almost a dead calm, and as she lay she saw little rabbits stealing out to play in the sunshine on the sands. She watched them running in circles like things on wheels and moving by clockwork. Then she closed her eyes, but still she saw them circling, circling, circling.

Then she was in the toy department of the Magazin du Louvre and a shop-woman was shewing her toy rabbits that ran in circles, five francs each.

She awoke at noon; the sore throat was gone, her bones no longer ached and the great beach lay under the heat of noon, humming like a stretched string to the touch of the sea.

Her left arm and side and thigh were scorched by the sun, but that was nothing; the sense of illness was gone, and her mind, quite clear and renewed, had regained its balance.

She remembered everything. La Touche was lying there in the cave, dead. The knife that had killed him she could see lying on the sand where she had dropped it; she had killed him. All these monstrous facts seemed old, settled and done with and of little more interest than the things and events of a year ago.

What seemed new was the beach and its desolation—its emptiness. It was as though a crowd of people had suddenly vanished from it; a crowd that any moment might return. The place seemed waiting and watching.

She cast her eyes towards the rocks of the Lizard Point and then towards the cave mouth; then hurriedly she began to put on her clothes, now dry and warm, and having dressed she stood for a moment again looking about her.

She could see the penguins in the distance going through their endless evolutions, and the rhythmical sound of the sea came from near and far mixed with the chanting and crying of the gulls. At any moment Bompard might appear labouring over those rocks, at any moment La Touche might step from the cave where he lay. That is what the beach told her, though she knew that the forms of the two men would appear no more; that she was here alone, utterly alone.

She took shelter from the sun in the men's cave. Bompard's tinder box was lying on the sand and half a box of Swedish matches. The men's blankets were tossed in a corner and the provisions and utensils were in their proper place. On a plate by the bags of biscuits lay the remains of the beef from last night's supper; she took it and ate it with a biscuit, sitting on the floor of the cave and staring before her out at the strip of beach where the boat lay on its side with the sea breaking beyond.

On the day the men had gone off inland on their expedition she had terrified herself with fancies of what it would be like were she to find herself here alone. Her imagination had gone far from the reality.

The thing had happened; the men were gone, gone forever, yet she was not alone. They filled the place by their absence far more than they had filled it by their presence.

The louder cry of a gull outside seemed hailing Bompard, the rustle of a rabbit on the sands seemed the coming of La Touche, the sound of the sea spoke of them, the boat seemed only waiting for them to launch it. They, whom a million years would not bring back.

She felt neither regret for the fate of La Touche nor sorrow for the fate of Bompard, all that seemed unreal, just as the darkness and terror of the night before seemed unreal. The real thing that touched her through everything was Expectancy. Expectancy, ghostly attenuated, yet ubiquitous.

It brought her to the cave mouth before she had finished her meal. The beach seemed to say to her: "Come out and look!" and she came out and looked, and the line of foam and the wheeling or stalking gulls held her for a moment as though saying—a moment, a moment more and you will see something. They will come. Any moment now you may see Bompard crossing the rocks. La Touche is not in that cave, he is here, everywhere.

She came back into the cave and sat down and finished her meal, the food had renewed her strength and with renewed strength her indifference to all that had happened began to pass.

She had killed La Touche. The reality of that fact was coming home to her now; she did not reason in the least on the matter saying he deserved to be killed, that had all been settled long ago in her mind, but the fact that she had killed him was standing strongly out before her, also the facts that he was dead and lying quite close to her and that though she did not mind his dead body she was beginning to dread something else.

Dead, he was beginning to frighten her just as he had frightened her when living. Then she found that it was just the same with Bompard. He was frightening her too.

Suppose one or the other were to peep in at her, and nod at her— she pictured it and then crushed the picture in her mind and got up and came out again and stood in the sun.

Then she came down to the boat and stood with her hand on the gunnel, and, for a moment as she stood thus, the terror of utter loneliness came to her in a hundred tongues and ways, and always with reference to the men who had vanished.

It was impossible to stay here alone—alone—absolutely alone; like a frightened child her mind appealed against this terror; it climbed the vacant skies and passed over the desolate hills in search of comfort. Was there a God? To whom could she run for comfort, for escape—?

As if in answer to her wild but unspoken question came a far-off roar brought on the wind from the great seal beach.

XVII

Friends in Desolation

She turned her face that way and stood for a moment with the faint breeze blowing her hair. Then she came running up the beach to the caves. In the men's cave she stood glancing rapidly about her like a person in a burning house seeking what he may save.

She picked up the tinder box and the box of matches and put them in her pocket. Then she began to remove everything from the cave. Making a sack of one of the blankets, she filled it with as much as she could drag along and brought it to the break in the cliffs where she dumped the contents.

It took her three journeys. Then, having collected everything in a big pile, she sat down for a moment to rest. The things would be safe here till she could fetch them to her new home, and the weather would not hurt them, except, maybe, the biscuits.

The thought of the biscuits troubled her, and the picture of them lying exposed in one of the torrential rains. Then she caught sight of a cleft in the basalt. It was dry and big enough to contain the bags and she placed them there having taken out some of their contents.

These and a couple of tins of meat she placed in one of the blankets, making a sack of it. Then she remembered the knife she had left lying on the sand before the cave where the dead man lay.

She fought against the idea of returning for it. Then her will made her go.

As she picked up the knife she glanced once again into the cave and once again caught a glimpse of the naked foot with the toe dug into the sand; then, placing the knife in its sheath and running like a frightened child she reached the break, caught up the sack, the extra blanket and the axe, which she had hidden among the bushes, and started.

It was not a heavy load, fortunately. Had it been heavy she would have dropped it, for, once moving, she had to run. The idea that she was deserting people who did not want to be deserted pursued her; now and again she stopped and turned for a moment—nothing; the Lizard rocks lay just the same and the beach and the forsaken boat, just the same, and the jeering gulls; yet, when she turned again to go on she had to run.

Near the great skull her right bootlace, getting loose, nearly tripped her. She sat down and tied it and then went on, walking now, but swiftly, till, nearing the river and in full sight of her new companions, she found herself suddenly free.

The hounds of Fear had given up the chase. The great sea elephants had driven them away. Here was no longer loneliness.

The great beasts sunning themselves on the flat rocks seemed more numerous and, as she crossed the river, a monster coming in from the sea in a thunder of foam saluted the land with a roar.

She recognized, or thought she recognized, the great bull that had followed her, he was lying, today, half-tilted to one side, he looked drunk with sun and laziness and as she came amongst them and sat down, as she had sat that day, she found that though a hundred pairs of eyes were watching her, scarcely a burly figure moved.

They had grown used to her, perhaps, or perhaps they recognized that she did not fear them now in the least, or that she had come for refuge and friendship.

Then she rose up and passing amongst them as a friend amongst friends came towards the caves in the basalt cliffs. They were smaller than the caves to the west but they were dry and free from water drip. She chose one and put her bundle down with the axe beside it.

PART III

XVIII

God Made Friendship

The place was as populous as a town. That was the soul-satisfying fact which she absorbed as she sat with the bundle and axe beside her. To be lonely here one would have to be deaf and blind and without the sense of smell. Now that their attention was no longer strained by watching her the great brutes filled the place with all sorts of sounds, grunts and grumbles, puffs and snorts like the escape of steam from a locomotive and now and then the flop of a great body changing position. There was another sound she got to know and recognize, after a while, the grumbling and rumbling of their interiors. Infested with sea-lice they were always scratching. Quite close to the cave mouth three great bulls were lying and every now and then one of them would turn and twist round and scratch himself with his flippers, the nearest bull had lost an eye in some past battle and they were all scarred about the necks, and seen close like this, in their natural state and as one of their company, the marvel of them, was beyond speaking.

She took off the oilskin coat and laid it on the sand of the cave, took the things from the blanket and spread the two blankets out and folded them. As she moved about she saw that the bulls had turned slightly, attracted by her movements, but they shewed not the slightest sign of mind disturbance. Then, having placed the things in order, she came out and walked down to the water's edge, making a detour now and then to avoid treading on the flippers or the tail of a monster. On coming amongst them a few minutes ago she had felt not the slightest fear, but this walk in cold blood from the cliff to the sea edge made her hold her breath. She felt as she had felt that first day when she sat down close to them. Angry, and with a sudden movement, one of these creatures could have destroyed her as a man destroys a fly; but she held on, and was rewarded.

Not one of them shewed any wish to destroy her, or anger, or uneasiness. They had accepted her into their company by not attacking or ejecting her, she ran counter to none of their desires or needs and evidently her form called up no recollections of the beast Man in their dim brains.

Then she was a female. Sex is more than a physical difference between one being and another, one can fancy it as one of the outstanding signs of the Wild to be read by instinct, as instinct reads the weather or season signs, or the sea mile posts that lead the seals and sea elephants thousands of leagues to strike some particular beach as an arrow strikes the bull's eye of a target.

The female, unless with young, is not dangerous to the male. One may fancy that amongst the few but burningly important warnings and directions in the book of Instinct.

Here, at the sea edge and within a few feet of the breaking waves, she sat down on a projecting rock and tried to measure with her eye the vast herd. The whole beach from where she sat to where the flat rocks ceased a mile and a half away on her right was spotted with them and she noticed that here and there they were always putting out to sea and coming ashore again.

Making for a spot on the right, a hundred yards from her she saw one coming ashore, swift as an arrow, steering with straight steadfast eyes and landing with the water cascading from his huge shoulders, whilst on the left one was putting out to sea in a burst of foam.

Then, of a sudden, all the shore edge bulls got in commotion slithering about, raising themselves on their flippers and blowing off steam.

A sea elephant was coming towards the beach, moving with a speed thrice that of any of the others, his head was raised and she could see the eyes that seemed blazing with wrath or challenge.

Then, as he came thundering on to the rocks, he lifted the echoes with a roar that resounded for miles along the beach.

All the others had landed in silence.

She did not know that this was a newcomer, a belated bull, held days behind the arrival of the others by some chance of the sea. Maybe he had hung fishing off the South Shetlands or the Horn, or beached for repairs after some sea fight off the Falklands; whatever had held him he was late.

He came swiftly up the rocks, casting his head from side to side but unchallenged. There were no females there yet to fight for and they evidently recognized him as one of the herd and not a stranger. The herd instinct, without which a nation would be a mob, ruled here and gave the belated one his place, and after a while of squattering about and sniffing and blowing he settled down with quieted eyes to rest. He had reached one of the stopping stages of his life, with the surety with which he would reach the last, on some desolate beach or reef of the sea.

The girl watched him. Not only did these new-found companions chase away loneliness and ghostly fears, but they brought her comfort. They seemed so sure, sure of food and life and the right to live, so undisturbed; it was as though she felt the presence of the ghostly shepherd who looks after the flocks of sea and land and who counts even the sparrows. She cast her eyes towards the islands and the sea-line; some day a ship would come and all this would be a dream of the past. She knew it. Her mind went back over all that she had been saved from—the wreck, the deathtraps and worst of all—La Touche. It was strange to think that a man should be worse than the others.

If that fisherman's knife had not been included in the gear of the boat!

It was now, as she sat thinking this and watching the huge harmless things around her, that a hatred of La Touche came into her mind, a hatred that seemed to have been waiting to enter until her mind was at rest. He seemed to her evil itself. He seemed to her connected with all the disasters that had happened and part of them. He had been the lookout on the *Gaston de Paris*, his quarrel had sent Bompard to his death, he had nearly unhinged her mind with terror. Had he possessed the evil eye? Then, for the first time, she recalled her premonition of disaster, yet, how she had refused to let the yacht be put off its course. They might now have been at New Amsterdam only for that. Yet it was not her fault. She had refused to alter the course, not for any selfish reason, quite the reverse, she had refused because she did not wish to spoil the plans of her host. It was Fate, not blind Fate, because the premonition was full sighted, it was Fate obeying some order. And it seemed to her that she could read in the order that she was to be saved. Why? God only knew, but so she read the facts, and she would be saved to the end and go back to the life she knew, or had known and die, perhaps, at last an old, old woman.

It seemed to her that this coming on to the sea elephant beach was a stage in her great journey that had brought her definitely nearer to the end of her loneliness. And whether all this were true knowledge or whether it was only the fancy of the ego its effect was to give her peace.

Then, as she sat there the strangest lonely figure on earth, she explored the pocket of her skirt and took the things from it. La Touche's knife, her rings knotted up in her handkerchief, the tobacco box of

Captain Slocum, the tinder-box and box of matches. Then she opened the tobacco box and re-read the purple writing with the tag "keep up your spirits." She could not visualize the old slab-sided whaling captain who had scrawled that, inspired no doubt by practical knowledge of disaster and the horrors of Kerguelen, but the message came now as an additional comfort, it seemed to her written by a hand other than that of man. She put the paper back in the box and, then, everything back in her pocket.

Then, like a stroke of humour, an incident occurred to lighten the whole beach.

A big platoon of penguins had crossed the river and marched up to the sacred precincts of the seal beach. Turning her head to see what the disturbance was about she sighted the penguins just at the end of their march and three bulls fronting them. The penguins wished to pass, either from impudence or a real desire to cross the beach, but the bulls barred the way, heading them off, turning and twisting, snorting as if to blow the feathered ones away.

The penguins bowed and scraped and explained, but the bulls, blind to politeness and deaf to argument only presented their heads, then they raised their rumps and made a half charge. The girl watched the penguins going at the double with heads slewed round as though fearful of their tails. Then she laughed.

The sea elephants had not only made her able to laugh, they had given her something to laugh over. Then came the thought: why had they refused the penguins and accepted her?

She did not know that the penguins were rival fishermen, she fancied that the sea elephants were somehow friendly to her, divining her friendship for them, and maybe she was right, though not perhaps in the way she fancied, for when God made friendship He made it out of queer and sometimes negative materials.

That night as she lay in her cave with a rolled-up blanket for pillow and the other blanket for covering, neither Ghosts nor Loneliness came to trouble her.

Two great bulls a few yards from the cave's mouth kept her warm and comfortable of mind.

She could hear their puffs and grunts and the occasional wobble-wobble of their digestive organs as they slept, dreaming maybe in their sleep, for sometimes they tossed and moved, and once one of them gave a "woof" as though trying to roar under the blanket of sleep.

She thought of dogs lying asleep; dogs dreamed and hunted in their dreams, why should not these?

Then suddenly the rain came down as though someone had pulled the string of a shower bath, but she knew that would not drive them away, guessing that rain to sea elephants was no more disturbing than sun to peaches.

Then she was chasing penguins along the beach, riding on a sea elephant towards that absolute oblivion which is the brand of sleep they serve at Kerguelen.

XIX

The Birds

It rained off and on for three days, but rain in Kerguelen is not the same as rain in England, just as rain at Windmere is not the same as rain at Birmingham. It does not depress, especially when you are busy. In those three days she made three journeys to the break in the cliffs to recover the things she had left there and she made her journeys, not to put too fine a point on it, with nothing on but the oilskin coat, the blanket she used for a sack got hopelessly soaked and her head was exposed to the rain owing to the fact that the sou'wester was in the cave where the dead man lay, but she got used to it, especially as neuralgia and colds are unknown in Kerguelen.

The loss of her only towel, the lump of cotton waste, was far worse than the loss of the sou'wester and would have been worse still only that she had other things to think about, especially on these journeys. They were terrible and required all her fortitude to make them, and they were terrible for a new reason. The birds had got at La Touche. Great predatory birds like cormorants thronged the beach opposite the cave, she could see them going in and out of the cave and she could hear them quarrelling in there in the darkness.

Then, on her last journey, as she was preparing to come back, happening to glance that way she saw a gull like a Burgomaster coming out of the cave mouth and pulling after it something long like a rope upon which the other gulls flung themselves. She turned and ran.

She had saved everything but one full bag of biscuits; she determined to leave them. If worst came to the worst there was bread stuff in the cache.

That night the memory of what she had seen haunted her sleep. It was as though La Touche, unable to get at her in the material world was determined to torment her in the imaginary.

She lay awake listening to the whale birds crying and the divers mewing and quarrelling like cats, then, dropping asleep, she was awakened at dawn by a new sound. Outside on the beach she heard a moaning like the voice of someone in pain.

She raised herself on her elbow. It was a human voice without any

HENRY DE VERE STACPOOLE

manner of doubt. It ceased, and springing to her feet she came out. But there was no human being on the beach, nothing but the bulky forms of the great sea bulls, and quite close to the cave a smaller form, a female that had landed during the night and had just given birth to a baby, a thing like a slug which she was fondling with her flippers.

Then in the strengthening light the girl could make out here and there on the beach the forms of other females, and by noon that day there were hundreds and hundreds, and on the next day the beach was one vast nursery. It was the first great act in the life history of these sea people towards which the girl's heart was going out more and more, and as she sat that day watching the mothers and their babies, and the great old bulls shuffling about like heavy fathers, sometimes she would smile and sometimes, sitting and watching, her mind would wander away lost and trying to grapple with the great mystery of which all this was only a part.

They were so human, so warm to the heart, and yet only a few days ago there was nothing here but the rocks and the cold and trackless sea. Then she noticed that today the bulls were not sunning themselves lazily, although the sun was out. They seemed disturbed, moving about aimlessly, lifting themselves on their flippers and now and then raising their short trunks.

Sometimes a female would make as if to get back to the sea but she was always headed off by a bull.

When dusk fell it seemed that the sentries were doubled, to judge by the noise of the flopping and moving about. The girl came to the cave entrance and looked, and lo and behold! every bull had cleared down towards the sea edge. She could see them stretching away into the dim distance, a hedge of vast forms broken and moving here and there, but always restored.

She thought that this line of defence was to keep the females back from the water, yet there seemed more than mere precaution at the bottom of the general disturbance that filled the beach. Then as she lay awake she could hear now and then a distant roar and once a big bull only a few hundred yards from the cave took it into his head to give tongue with a blast like the first deep "woof" of a siren, then came another sound quite close to the cave entrance, a sound like the broken lapping of ripples, interrupted by movements and little snorts and sighs. It was a baby seal sucking away at the teats of its mother. The pair was just outside the cave.

XX

Væ Victis

A Howling wind that rose at midnight carrying niagaras of rain oversea from the mountains sank at dawn leaving a clear sky and a falling sea.

As she came out into the early morning light she could see boosts of spray all along the rocks, but by the time she had tidied things up and finished her breakfast these had vanished and the water was coming in, rolling lazily, and the sounds of the breakers came sleepy and evenly spaced as though ruled by a metronome.

The bulls no longer lined the shore, though keeping close to the water they had broken up into groups, yet still the sense of disturbance was there pervading the beach like an atmosphere.

The tide was just turning back from the flood, and as she stood watching she noticed the curious fact that not a single bull was taking to the water; ordinarily, here and there along the rocks, there was always some monster taking a header, some vast bulk beaching in a potter of foam. This morning there was nothing of this sort.

Picking her way between the mothers and their babies she came down to the sea edge, choosing a broad space left vacant because of the bad landing conditions. The rocks here were higher, forming a miniature cliff some four or five feet in height and from this point looking seaward something caught her eye.

Three black objects moving in a line were making a long ripple on the swell. They were the heads of three sea elephants moving like one. Then the line became the segment of a circle bending in shore. But the swimmers were not going to land; they kept parallel to the rocks and a few hundred yards out, and as they passed she could see clearly the great heads and sometimes the massive shoulders rising and washing away the water and the eyes, as the heads swung now and then shorewards, wicked eyes that seemed to blaze with the light of anger or battle.

She was not alone in observing them. They had been spotted by a trumpet-voiced sentry and instantly the whole place was in commotion. The air split with a roar that passed along from section to section of the beach whilst the cliffs resounded and a thousand sea-gulls rose as if from nowhere, crying, cat-calling and making a snowstorm in the sunlight.

On the roar and as if destroyed by it the three heads vanished.

Then, far out, they reappeared, only to dive again, leaving the sea blank, but for a school of porpoises passing along on their quiet business a mile away towards the east.

The girl sat watching. There was something in all this of greater import than the appearance of three swimming sea elephants. The beach told her that. Not a bull in all that vast herd but was in motion, either helping to crowd the females back towards the cliffs or patrolling the rocks. She could see them here and there rising up on their hind-quarters as though to get a better view of the sea. They reminded her of dogs begging for biscuits. Then, turning her eyes seaward again she saw a black spot; it was a moving head. Then another broke the surface and another, till in a moment, and for a mile-long stretch, hundreds of heads appeared, all driving shorewards and then dipping and vanishing only to reappear still closer in and closing on the beach with the swiftness of destroyers.

Then she knew, and, springing up, turned to run; but her retreat was cut off towards the caves by the females herded up and, before she could collect her thoughts, the army of invasion was flinging itself from the water, and the whole sea beach from end to end was filled with the thunder of battle.

For days the lone bulls had been cruising at sea waiting and watching till all the females were on shore under guard of their husbands. So it happened every year as now, ending in a battle for the possession of wives, a battle waged without quarter and with a fury whose sound reached the echoes of the hills.

Safe on the little rock plateau she watched the thunderous onslaught, frightened and then terrified and crying out.

The invaders drove in from the sea like the sweep of a curved sword. They struck the beach first a mile away and the battle ran towards her like fire along tinder, boomed towards her ever loudening till it broke to right and left where the sea bulls flung themselves on the rocks and the land bulls charged the on-comers like battering rams. Some were hurled back, only to return again, others held their ground. Then the real business began whilst the ground trembled and the air shook and the rocks poured blood.

Round her, and for a mile away, they fought like rams and they fought like dogs and they fought like tigers, and over the roaring siren sounds of the fight the gulls flew like the fume of it, screaming and swooping and circling in spirals, and through everything like the continuous thud-thud of a propeller came the dunch of tons of flesh meeting tons of flesh head on, shoulder on, or side on.

She saw bulls ripped beyond belief, with shoulders slashed as if by the down strokes of a sword, yet still fighting as though untouched, with rumps raised and tails up and teeth in the necks of their enemies, one had his eye torn out, yet tremendous and victorious he was literally punching his antagonist back into the sea.

The foam broke red and suddy; she saw that, just as she had seen the name of the *Albatross* in the tremendous moment of the great ship's eclipse, and, just as the name, the red breaking foam seemed to concentrate in itself the whole terror of the business.

Then, standing like a person helpless in a dream during the full hour that the battle raged, she saw the females break bounds and spread over the rocks carrying or pushing their young as if to get closer to the fight, and then she saw the battle beginning to break. Here and there bulls beaten and done for were taking to the sea and over all the beach the fight had spread inwards towards the cliffs. The sea bulls were beating the land bulls as a whole, interpenetrating them, getting closer to the females, herding the vanquished out.

And she saw, now, as though a curtain had been raised, that the whole great battle was between individuals.

The bulls fresh from the sea though attacking *en masse* were under the dominion of no enmity in common, each had come to find a rival and having found him had no eyes for anything else. Nor having once conquered did he pursue.

Another, and a wonderful thing, shewed up: the females had grouped themselves as if to be taken, and now on the clearing beach could be seen family parties, some under the dominion of their new lords and masters, some still being fought for.

So it hung, dwindling little by little till at last only two warriors were left like the last-blazing point of the fight.

They were the biggest of the two herds; they looked as though they had been rolled in gore and they seemed equally furious and equally exhausted. All their rage was in their eyes. Too beaten to bite they could only boost one against another like two schoolboys trying to push one another off a form.

It seemed a miserable and tame ending of their tremendous struggle

HENRY DE VERE STACPOLE

and she recognized, or thought she recognized, that the biggest of them was the bull who had followed her that day like a dog towards the river.

This shouldering and pushing was his last effort to hold to his wife and family. In war it is the last step that counts, could he make it? Then a strange thing happened. The two monsters paused in their pushing, relaxed, and seemed for a moment to forget the existence of one another. That tremendous weariness lasted for a minute and then they woke up and the biggest bull began to shuffle off to the sea.

His heart or his mind had failed him. The closer he got to the water's edge the swifter he moved and the plunge of his body into the water was the last sound of that battle.

Not a corpse lay on the beach, nothing but the victorious lords and their ladies, and the lords seemed to pay as little attention to their ghastly wounds as they did to their old or newly got wives, who, now that peace was restored, were busy suckling their young.

A queer people, humorous and terrifying, making the girl feel that she had placed her hand on something likeable, almost lovable, that had yet, of a sudden, nearly frightened her to death.

She sat recovering herself and helped by the regiment of penguins who marched up to the seal beach and, knowing better than to attempt to cross it, stood bowing to the world in general and talking one to the other perhaps on the horrors of war.

PART IV

XXI

Time Passes

I t is not good to be alone. As the weeks passed she began to lose and forget the feeling of surety in rescue and at times, now, she found herself talking out loud, putting what was in her mind into speech as though a companion were by, and sometimes she would hear a voice hallooing to her and start and cast her eyes over the desolate beach only to see the gulls.

The beach was always haunted by queer noises; the chanting sound of the waves coming in, a faint sound like the beating of a drum at very low tide, to say nothing of the booming of bitterns and the barking of brent geese and the hundred voices of the wind. She would listen and listen, her mind wandering aimlessly, and in the great rains, when the whole sea was shut out by the downpour, the noise would lull her like opium.

The baby sea elephants lost their long black coats and put on their suits of fine yellow fur and took themselves to the nursery by the river, where all day long they played and tumbled and swam, and then she would sit and watch them like a mother watching her children.

The great battle of the bulls seemed like something far away beyond which other things were becoming vague. Something that was not meant to be seen so close by human eyes, something that had pushed her still further from man.

It was full summer now, the season of tremendous sunsets and when the sky was clear, vast conflagrations lit themselves beyond the Lizard Point painting the islands and purpling the skies, and one evening as she sat in the western blaze watching the moving beach and listening to the playing and quarrelling of the nursery a voice said to her:

"Some day all these will take to the sea and leave you. There will be nothing here but the rocks and the sea."

It was as though the sunset had spoken.

The thought aroused her as a knock on the door arouses a sleeper. Fighting against it her mind became more fully awake. She said to herself: "If they go I will go too."

For a long time now she had lived without hot food or drink. On coming here first she had cut some wood from the figure-head to make a fire, but it was damp, just damp enough to prevent it from kindling, so she had let things go as women do in the matter of food when they have not anyone else to feed; she had burrowed into the cache and got at some of the tins of vegetables and on these and biscuits and tinned meat she made out, eating less and less as time went on.

It is bad to be alone, even with sea elephants to ward off fears, even with provisions enough for a year and a cave to shelter one.

She had never given in. She had fought the future and refused to be frightened by it, she had worked for life and taken refuge in the moment, and now the moment was taking its revenge for being too much lived in.

To eat was almost too much trouble and presently the seal nursery became too long a walk and the little sea elephants at play had lost their power to interest her. Sleep began to take the place of food and sometimes, and for no reason, she would weep like a child.

The food she ate sometimes seemed to poison her, bringing on vomiting and dysentery, and it poisoned her because her stomach failed to digest it.

She was being poisoned, poisoned by loneliness. Had her stomach not failed her mind would have given, as it was the weakness of malnutrition saved her reason as it slowly destroyed her hold on life.

Her dreams became sometimes more vivid than reality and they always held her to the beach where she watched without terror battles between monstrous sea elephants and processions of penguins infinite in length, penguins that passed her bowing, bowing, bowing till she woke in the dark with the palms of her hands dry and burning and her lips like pumice stone and her tongue feeling hard like the tongue of a parrot, but the worst experience of all was a shock that came nearly everytime she lay down at night and just before sleep took her.

It seemed like the blow of a fist, a fist that hit her everywhere, making her start and draw up her legs and cry out.

All this, perhaps, was what she had foreseen when long ago she had watched a great ship that had told her of Desolation—and something worse.

This was what no one had ever imagined in connection with Desolation. Its power to kill with its own hand. To gently destroy,

HENRY DE VERE STACPOOLE

sucking the vitality like a vampire and fanning the victim to dullness with its wings.

The sea elephants might have noticed that the female creature to whom they had grown so accustomed appeared little now, a shrinking vision that everyday shortened its wanderings; that it walked differently, that it seemed more bent. But the sea elephants knew nothing of Loneliness or its works, nor did they notice, one morning, that though the sun was shining the figure did not appear at all.

XXII

A Newcomer

One morning, brilliant, with the deceptive brilliancy of Kerguelen, a big man, rough and red-bearded and carrying a bundle slung over his shoulder, stood on the rocks that formed the eastern point of the great beach; the sun was at his back and before him lay the seven mile stretch of sand and rock leading to the far-off Lizard Point.

He was over six feet in height but so strongly built that he scarcely looked his inches. He was a sailor. The gulls might have told that by the way he stood, and his eyes, accustomed to roving over vast spaces, swept the beach before him from end to end, took in the sea elephants moving like slugs and the seal-nursery and the river and the sands beyond and the Lizard Point crawling out to sea beyond the sands.

Then he cast his eyes inland.

He wanted to get to the west and he had to choose between seven miles of broken country or seven miles of easy beach.

The sea elephants were a bar across the beach. He could gauge their size from where he stood, they looked formidable, but they were less so than the rocks strewing that broken country. He had climbed over rocks and gone round rocks and nearly fallen from rocks till rocks had become in his mind enemies bitter, brutal, callous, and far more formidable than live things. He chose the beach and came down to it, taking his way along the sea edge as a person takes his way along a pavement edge, giving possibly turbulent people the wall.

As he closed up towards the seal beach he kept his eyes fixed on the great bulls and their families, and the bulls, as he drew closer, shifted their position to watch him, beyond that they shewed no sign. Then as he began to pass them he recognised that he had nothing to fear, the females alone, here and there, shewed any sign of disturbance, shuffling towards him with wicked eyes, rising on their flippers, but always sinking down and shuffling back as he went on.

Further along, though followed and met by a hundred pairs of eyes, even the females began to treat him with indifference. It was as though the whole herd were under the dominion of one brain that recognized him as harmless and passed him along. He would pause now and then to look at them with the admiration of strength for strength. He was of their type, a bull man, rough from the sea as themselves.

Then he saw the caves and would have passed them only for something that caught his eye. A red labelled Libby tin was lying on the dark sand close to the mouth of one of the caves, and if you wish to know how an old tomato tin or an old beef tin can shout, you must go alone to the great beach of Kerguelen and find one there—which you will not.

The sight of the tin made him start and catch in his breath. The tin was everything he knew of ships and men focussed in a point, a knight in armour riding along the beach would have astonished him no more, would have heated his blood far less.

He struck up towards it, took it in his hand, examined it inside and out and then cast his eye at the cave before which it had lain. He saw something in the cave, it was a woman; a woman lying on the sand with a rolled-up blanket under her head. She was lying on her back and he saw a thin white hand, so small, so thin, so strange that he drew slightly back, glanced over his shoulder, as if to make sure that everything was all right with the world, and then glanced again, drawing closer.

Then he called out and the woman moved. He could see her face now, white, and thin and drawn, and great eyes, terrible eyes, fixed on him.

Away out at sea, terribly near the coast of Death she saw him, a living being, as the castaway sees a ship on the far horizon.

He saw her hold out her arms to him and then, throwing his bundle aside, he was down on his knees beside her, holding the hands that sought his and with those terrible eyes holding him too.

He saw her lips moving, saw that they were dry and parched. Then he knew. She wanted water.

An empty baling tin was lying near her. The sight of the river close by was in his mind, he released the hands, picked up the tin and scrambled out of the cave. As he ran to the river heedless of sea elephants or anything else he kept crying out: "Oh, the poor woman. Oh, the poor woman." He seemed like a huge thing demented. The baby sea elephants scuttered out of his way and as he came running back he spilt half the contents of the tin. Then he was down beside her again, dipping his finger in the water and moistening her lips.

She sucked his finger as a baby sucks and the feel of that made him curse with the tears running down into his beard. The size of the baling tin seemed horrible beyond words; he couldn't get it to her lips. Still he went on, not knowing that it was his finger that was giving her back life; the blessed touch of a human being that had come almost too late.

He was sitting on his heels, and now, casting his great head from side to side, he saw things stacked behind her, tins and a bag and metal things that shone dimly. Putting out his hand he caught a corner of the bag. It was a bread bag, sure enough, and as he pulled it towards him the other things came clattering down almost hitting her, and amongst them, God-sent, a little tin spoon.

He seized it and filled it and brought the tip to her lips and she swallowed the water making movements with her throat muscles as though it were half a cupful. He did this a dozen times and then rested, spoon in hand, watching her. She made a couple of slight movements with her head as if nodding to him and her eyes never left him for a moment, they seemed holding on to life through him. He offered a spoonful of water again, she moved her head slightly as though she had had enough, but her eyes never left him.

He knew. If the whole thing had been carefully explained to him he could not have known better how she was clinging to him, as a child to a mother, as a creature to life. And all the time his rough mind in a tumble of confusion and trouble was trying to think how she came like this, with a bread bag close to her and a river within reach.

A tin cup had come down with the other things, it gave him an idea, and getting a biscuit out of the bag he broke it up, put the pieces in the cup with some water and let them soak. It took a long time and all the while, now and then, he kept talking to her.

"There. Y'aren't so bad after all—keep up till I get you something more. There's no use in troubling—you'll be on your pins soon."

He would pause to swear at the biscuit for not softening quicker, helping it to crumble with his mighty thumb thrust in the cup. To "get food into her" was his main idea, it didn't matter about thumbs. He was not without experience of starvation and thirst and what they can do to people, and, as he worked away talking to her, pictures from the past came to him of people he had seen like this, nearly "done in" by the sea.

Then he began to feed her with the noxious pap. He managed to get six spoonfuls "into her" and then he saw she would stand no more; still, that was something, and as he brooded on his heels watching her he saw that she was making a struggle to keep it down, and he knew that if she brought it up she was done for. And all the time she kept holding him with her eyes as though he were helping her in the struggle.

He was. The sight of him gave her just the strength necessary to tide over the danger point; then she lay still and the food, such as it was, began to do its work.

One may say that the stomach thinks; every mood of the mind can touch it and it can influence every mood of the mind.

Then the terrible fixed eyes began to grow more human, then to close slightly. She was still far at sea, but no longer adrift; like a little boat taken in tow she was heading now back for the shore. She fell asleep holding his thumb.

The bits of wood she had chipped from the figure-head were lying in a little heap near the cave mouth and the axe lay beside them. He noted them as he sat motionless as a carved figure till the grip on his thumb relaxed, and the dry claw-like hand, now growing moist and human, gave up its hold.

Then, crawling out, stealthily and side-ways like a crab, he seized the axe and, rising up outside, axe in hand, stood looking in at the woman. He stood watching her, making sure that she was well asleep, then he turned towards the seal nursery swinging the axe. There he murdered a little girl sea elephant after a short, sharp chase over the rocks. Then, close to the caves and with his sailor's knife, he stripped her of fur and blubber. He placed the blubber on one side, cut up the meat and retaining the heart and kidneys wrapped the head and the remainders in the pelt and dumped them in a crack in the rocks.

Having done this he went to the river and washed his hands free of the blood and grease.

In his bundle there was a box with half a dozen matches, they would have been gone long ago only that long ago his tobacco had given out. They were useful now.

He knelt down and undid the bundle. There was in it beside the match-box a shirt rolled up, two sailors' knives, two tobacco boxes, a couple of huge biscuits, a piece of sail cloth and a pair of men's boots, one might have fancied from the knives and tobacco boxes that he was the only survivor of a party of three cast on the coast and that he had kept these things as relics. That was the fact.

When he had secured the matches his next thought was of the firewood and the baling tin. There was a saucepan away at the back of the cave under the other things but he could not see it. He could see the tin but he dreaded going in to get it lest he should wake the woman and she should clutch his thumb again.

That was a bad experience and he told himself that if she had not relaxed her hold he would have been sitting there still tied hand and foot and not daring to move—strength in the clutch of weakness, to whom God has given a power greater that that of strength.

He crawled in and secured the tin without wakening her and as much firewood as he wanted. It was fairly dry and with the help of the blubber he soon had it burning between two big stones, then he put the tin on, half filled with water, and dropped in the seal meat cut fine. He was making soup for himself as well as for her. He had been without hot food for ages and the smell of the stuff as it began to cook made him sometimes forget her entirely.

Predatory gulls had found the pelt and the head in the rock crevice and their quarrelling filled the beach. He turned his head sometimes to look at them as he sat squatting like a gipsy before the little fire, tilting the tin by the handle and stirring the contents with his knife. He was a man of resource for, before filling the tin with fresh water, he had dipped it in the sea so as to get some salt into the mess.

Then when the stuff was cooked, having no spoon, he had to wait until it cooled a bit before tasting it. He went to the cave mouth to have a look at the woman. The quarrelling of the great gulls had evidently awakened her, for her eyes were open, and as his figure cut the light at the cave entrance her head moved. He ran back for the precious tin and, carrying it carefully, and half carried away by the entrancing smell of it, knelt down beside her, then picking up the spoon began to feed her before feeding himself.

XXIII

RAFT

It took him three days to bring her back safe to life. It poured with rain during those three days but he managed to light little fires in one of the caves with seal blubber and routing out the things in her cave he found everything she had so carefully salved, the cups and plates, the tin of coffee, half empty now—everything, even to the tobacco the men had taken from the cache, he found Bompard's tinder-box and the Swedish match box belonging to La Touche. He had given the woman life and she had given him tobacco and sometimes, sitting in the adjoining cave and smoking between nursing times, he would bring his big fist down on his thigh, just that.

Here was a woman starving to death and dying of thirst with food enough for a ship's company at her elbow. And the tobacco! Where was the explanation? She was able to speak a little now. She had spoken at first in French, which he could not understand, then she spoke in English as good as his; another mystery. A woman all gone to pieces that spoke two tongues and was different somehow from any woman he had ever known.

Then the things she had said: "Who are you? I am not dreaming this? Are you really, really, truly—Oh, *don't* leave me." Crazy talk like that. And it was always "Oh, don't leave me." Then he would lay his pipe down carefully on the sand of the cave and pass through the sheeting rain to have a look at her. Sometimes she would have dozed off and he could get back to his pipe, sometimes she was awake and then he would have to sit down beside her and hold her hand and stroke it or play with her fingers just as one plays with the fingers of a child. At these moments he was transformed, he was no longer a man, he was a mother, and the hand that could break down the resistance of a bellying sail was the hand of a child. He no longer thought of her as the "poor woman," an infant is sexless, so did she seem, or so would she have seemed had he thought of the matter. He didn't. As a matter of fact thought was not his strong suit in the game of life. He was a man from the world of Things. That was why, perhaps, he made such a good sick nurse. He did not fuss, nor talk, his touch was firm, firm as his determination to "get food into her" and his hand, big as a ham, was delicate because it was the hand of a perfect steersman. It was used to handling women in the form of three thousand ton ships, coaxing them, humouring them—up to a point.

He fed her now from one of the tin cups. Every two hours of the day, unless she was asleep, half a cupful of food went into her whether she liked it or not; "hot stuff," for though the firewood was done he found that the blubber alone was the best fuel in the world.

On the second day she was able to raise herself up, and once when he came in he found that she had been moving about the cave and that she had rearranged the blanket that did for a pillow.

Then on the morning when the blessed sun shone she was able to come out and sit on a patch of sand with one of the blankets for a rug.

She looked old and worn, but no longer terrible, and as she sat with her thin hands folded in her lap watching the great sea bulls and the cows, as if contemplating them for the first time, the man who had helped her out and placed her there was at a loss—she was a sight to inspire pity in a savage. He took his seat beside her on a piece of rock and rolling some tobacco in his hand stuffed his pipe.

"You're all right now," said he.

She nodded her head and smiled.

"Yes," she said, "this is good."

"Lucky I came along," he said, "wouldn't have seen you only an old tin hit my eye."

He put the pipe in his pocket, got up, went to the cave where he did the cooking and came back with a cup half full of coffee and half a biscuit.

"Dip it in," said he.

She did as she was bid. It was the first time he had given her coffee and the stimulant brought a flush to her cheeks and cheered her heart so that she began to talk.

"There are more biscuits in a place down the beach," she said, "and down there," she nodded to the left, "there are a lot of things hidden under a heap of stones. It's beyond the river on the left."

Then the empty cup began to shake in her hand and he took it from her.

"You're not over strong yet," said he, "but you'll be better in a bit with this sun. Y'aren't afraid of the sea cows, are you?"

She shook her head.

"Thought you wouldn't be," said he, "there's no harm in them. Well, I'll be moving about. I'll go and have a look down the beach and see what's to be found."

He hung for a moment with the cup in his hand shading his eyes and looking seaward, then he turned towards the cave to put the cup back.

"What is your name?" she said, suddenly, bringing him to a halt.

"Raft," said he.

"Raft," she repeated the name several times in a low voice as if committing it to memory or turning it over in her mind.

"How long might you have been here?" he asked, standing in a doubtful manner, as though debating in his mind the wisdom of allowing her to strain her strength answering questions.

"I don't know," said she, "a long while. I was wrecked with two men from a yacht. The *Gaston de Paris*. We came here in a boat. They are both dead."

At the name *Gaston de Paris* Raft nodded his head. Already a suspicion that she might be one of the yacht's crowd had come into his mind, so the news came scarcely as a surprise.

"It was us you hit," said he, "I'm one of the chaps from the old hooker."

"The *Albatross*?"

"That's her."

She said nothing for a moment, looking away over at the islands. She could see the name, still, written as if on the night. Then she remembered the boat sail she had seen when adrift with Bompard and La Touche.

"There were four of us got off," said he, "we struck them islands over there and put in but there was nothing but rocks in that part. Next day we put out, but got blown down the coast; we got smashed landing; all but a chap named Ponting and me went under, but one chap's body was hove up and we stripped him. I've got his boots and his knife in that bundle over there in the cave, and Ponting's. We saved a bag of bread."

He took his seat again on the rock and, placing the cup beside him, took the pipe from his pocket, but he did not light it. He held it, rubbing the bowl reflectively. He seemed to have come to an end of his story.

"Did the other man die?" she asked.

"He went getting gulls' eggs one day," said Raft, "and slipped over the cliff. They're big, the cliffs, down there. I found him all broke up on the rocks. He didn't live more than a minute when I got to him and I had to leave him; the tide was coming up."

"Poor man," said she.

He rose up and, taking the cup, stood for a moment again looking seaward.

"Well, I'll be off down the beach," said he, "you won't be frightened to be here by yourself?"

"No," she replied, "but don't go very far."

"I'll keep in sight," said Raft.

He put the cup in the cave and off he went whilst she sat watching him; everything, life itself, seemed centred in him. A terrible feeling came over her at moments that he might vanish, that, looking away for a moment and turning again she might find him gone and nothing but the beach and the gulls.

Beyond the river he turned and saw her watching him and waved his hand as if to reassure her. She waved in reply and then sat watching till he reached the figure-head and stood to examine it.

He seemed very small from here. She saw him standing and looking inland, he had seen the cache, no doubt, and he would want to go to it; if he did that he would disappear from sight. But he did not go to it, he kept on always in view, exploring the rocks and the sands and stopping now and then as if to look back.

It seemed to her that he could read her mind and feel her terror of being left alone. Then her mind went back over the last few days.

She had been very near death. She had drunk the last of the water in the tin and had been too feeble to go for more. What had brought her to that pass? It seemed to her that the rocks, the sea and the sky had slowly sucked her vitality away from her till at last she could not eat, could not walk, could not think. All that time her mind had never thought of loneliness, the thing that was killing her had veiled itself by numbing her brain and weakening her body. But near death her mind had cleared and the great grief of desolation stood before her. Then God-sent, a form had pushed the grief aside and a hand had taken her lonely hand and a finger had moistened her lips. But it was the knowledge that the hand was a real hand that gave her the first lead back to life.

Then the last three days. The feeling of extreme helplessness and sickness and the knowledge that she was watched over and cared for and thought for—there was no word to express what all that meant. It turned the great rough figure to a spirit, great and tender and benign.

HENRY DE VERE STACPOOLE

He was coming along back now carrying something he had picked up amongst the rocks. It was a crab.

A great satisfactory two pound crab bound up in kelp ribbon so craftily that it could neither bite nor escape. He put it on the sand for her to look at before taking it off to boil.

The sun was hot and as he stood whilst she admired his prize: "Don't you feel the sun to your head?" asked he.

"No," she replied, "I like it. I had a hat—a sou'wester but it's in a cave away down the beach. There's a dead man there."

"A dead man?" said Raft.

"Yes. I killed him."

"Killed him?"

"It was partly accident. He was one of the sailors. He was a bad man. The other sailor got lost and never came back and I was left alone with this man. He nearly frightened me to death."

"Swab," said Raft.

"Then one night he crawled into my cave in the dark and I struck out with the knife and it killed him—he's lying there now. I didn't mean to kill him, but he frightened me."

"Swab," said Raft, two tones deeper. Then he laughed as if to himself. "Well, that's a go," said he. He took a pull at his beard as he contemplated this slayer of men seated on her blankets at his feet. She glanced up and saw that he was laughing and a wan smile came around her eyes, it seemed to him like a glimmer of sunshine from inside of her. Then bending down he pulled up the blanket that had slipped from her left shoulder and settled it in its place.

"I'll tell you all about it sometime," said she, "when I feel stronger."

"Ay, ay," said Raft. Then he went off with the crab to boil it.

As he attended to this business in the cave, half-sitting, half-kneeling before the little fire, he chuckled to himself now and then, and now and then he would bring his great hand down on his thigh with a slap.

The idea of her killing a man seemed to him the height of humour. He didn't put much store on men's lives in general, and none at all on the life of an unknown swab who deserved his gruel. Then he was of the type that admires a fighting thing much more than a peaceful and placid thing, and he felt the pleasure of a man who has rescued a seemingly weak and inoffensive creature only to find that it has pluck and teeth of its own.

She had gone up a lot in his estimation. Besides, her feebleness and forlorn condition had wounded him in a great soft part of his nature where the hurt felt queer. This new knowledge somehow eased the hurt. He could think of her now apart from her condition and think more kindly of her, for the strange fact remains that the very weakness and forlornness that had wakened his boundless compassion had antagonized him. When he had found the crab the idea had come to him that here was some different sort of food to "put into her"; he was thinking that same thought now but with more enthusiasm. Yes, she had gone up a lot in his estimation.

XXIV

A Dream

This same Raft whom the fo'c'sle could subdue to the surroundings, making him as faithful a part of the picture as the kerosene lamp, on the beach stood immense both in size and significance.

It was as though the fo'c'sle had the power to dwindle him, the beach, to expand him.

The girl had never seen him in the fo'c'sle so she could not appreciate the difference that environment made in him, and perhaps she saw him ever so slightly magnified, but it seemed to her that he was big enough to form part of the landscape, that he was one with the seven mile beach and the Lizard Point and the great islands and the sea elephants.

Not only had she been crushed down by loneliness; size had helped. Raft seemed to reduce the size of things, so that the seven mile strand and the vast islands and sea spaces no longer burdened her, and in some magical way whilst he reduced the proportions of his surroundings they increased his potency and significance. He was in his true setting, part of a vast picture without a frame.

It was not alone his physical dimensions. Bompard had been a big man, but Bompard could not fill that beach. No, it was something else—what we call, for want of a better expression, "the man himself."

Then there was another thing about him, he found food of all sorts where Bompard and La Touche had found nothing; he brought in crabs and cray-fish and penguins eggs, he brought down rabbits with stones. That was his great art. A stone in the hand of Raft was a terrible missile and his aim was deadly.

At the end of a week the girl was able to accompany him along the beach to the cache where he unearthed some stores and came upon the harpoon which he carried back with them.

Then one day he suddenly appeared before her carrying her lost sou'wester. He had gone off down the beach in the direction of the Lizard Point and he came back carrying the hat in his hand. He must have been into the cave where the remains of La Touche lay, but he said nothing about that.

It was nearly a fortnight since she had told him of how she had lost it and he must have treasured the fact up in his mind all that time.

The weather had cleared again, after a tremendous blow from the south, and as they sat that evening in the sunset blaze before the caves, Raft, who had been staring steadfastly out to sea as if watching something, began to talk.

"That chap Ponting told me this side of the coast is no use for ships," said he. "They keep beyond them islands for fear of the reefs. I reckon the old sea cows know that or there wouldn't be so many on this beach. He said there was a bay round to the westward where ships put in."

"How far?" asked the girl.

"A goodish bit," replied Raft. "I was making for that bay when I struck you. I was thinking," he finished, "that when you were stronger on your pins we might make for there."

"Leave here?"

"Ay," said Raft, "there's not much use sticking here."

She said nothing for a moment, she felt disturbed.

Since her recovery she had fallen into a state of quietude. She who had been the leader of Bompard and La Touche, she who had fought and worked so determinedly for existence had now no ambition, no desire for anything but rest. The strength of this man who had given her back her life seemed a shield against everything, just as a wall is a shield against the wind; she was content to sit in its shelter and rest. The idea of new exertions and unknown places terrified her.

"But how are you to know the bay?" asked she, "there may be a good many bays along the coast."

"No," said Raft, "Ponting told me there wasn't a decent anchorage but this. He said this bay wasn't to be mistook, looks as if it was cut out with a spade and the cliffs run high and black, there's a seal beach that way and it's after seals the ships come. Well, there's time enough to think of it seeing you are not fit to move yet."

"Oh, I'll soon be all right," said she. "I'm getting stronger everyday."

"What gets me," said Raft, "is how you fell to pieces like that, with all that stuff at your elbow and a river close by."

"It was being alone," replied she, "I did not know it at the time, but I got so that I did not care to eat and then at last I believe I didn't eat anything at all. I couldn't have imagined that just being alone would make a person like that. You see I had food and water. If I had been compelled to hunt about for food I expect I would have been all right, as it was I had nothing to do and was just driven in on myself."

Raft said nothing for a moment, he was turning this over in his mind. He could not understand it. The idea of a person with plenty of food and a good set of teeth dying of starvation just because she was lonely seemed to him outrageous, yet he knew she was speaking the truth. It was another strange thing about this strange woman. She was altogether strange, different from any human being he had ever met and growing more different everyday now that she was "filling out," and getting her voice back.

That voice, soft and musical and refined, had disturbed the sea elephants when she first talked to them as people talk to horses and dogs, it was something they had never heard before in the language of tone, and so it was with this sea animal with a red beard. He could not tell whether he liked it or not, never asked himself the question, it was part of her general strangeness and to be considered along with her clinging, man killing and double-tongued qualities, also with the fact that she had starved almost to death because she was alone; also with her eyes and new face, for she was growing younger looking everyday and better looking, and her eyes, naturally lovely, were growing natural again.

As he looked at her now sitting in the sunset this return of beauty struck him as it almost might have struck the sea elephants. It pleased him. Had he put his thoughts into words he would have said that she was filling out and getting more pleasant looking. At her very best he would never have tacked the word beauty on to her; a buxom, rotund, beady-eyed young female would have made the word beauty spring to his lips—Cléo de Bromsart, never. But she was getting more pleasant looking and her eyes were getting over their "stiffness"—which was something, and he felt pleased.

Presently, alone in his cave, he would bring his fist down on his thigh with a bang and chuckle over her contrarieties, reviewing her against that terrific picture he had seen in the cave when he had gone to fetch the sou'wester; the picture of a man who had been torn to pieces by Burgomasters and cormorants. It had been necessary to wash the sou'wester for a long time in sea water before bringing it back.

She had done that chap in proper; the work of the gulls and the work of the girl were hardly dissociated in his mind—there was the Result. Just as though a baby had smashed a rock with its fist. Hence the chuckles, heightened by her clinging ways, her fragility, her musical voice, her starvation due to loneliness, her double tongue, her unaccountable tricks of manner.

And she, as she sat in the sunset not knowing his thoughts, had you asked her how she felt about him would have answered with steadfast eyes that she loved him. Meaning that she loved him as she had learned to love the sea-elephants, or as she would have loved a great carthorse that had stood between her and danger, or a huge dog. She scarcely thought of him as a man—just as a great benign thing, human, but nearer to the heart than any human being life had brought her in contact with till now.

Her almost passionate gratitude had little to do with this measure of him; any kindly man might have done what he had done. It was perhaps the feeling of his great strength, of his possible fierceness that gave the touch of benignity to him.

"Weren't you afraid of them sea cows?" said he at last, "you must have come clean through them to get to that cave."

"No," she replied, "I didn't mind them, quite the reverse. I came here because of them."

"Because of them!"

"Yes. They were company."

"Meaning—"

"Friends."

"Y'mean to say—friends did you call them? Well, I don't know, there's no accountin'."

He hung in irons. So she had been keeping company with the sea cows—and she talked of them as "friends."

Now Raft, for all his limitless power of compassion for a female in distress would have slaughtered those same "sea-cows" to the last bull, and without a shred of compunction or compassion, had he possessed kettles to boil down the blubber and a vessel to carry the oil. He had already done in two of the babies for food when she was not looking. The idea of talking about them as friends tickled his mind in a new place. Then, as he glanced at the great bulls taking headers in the sunset light and snorting in from the sea and squatting over the beach, he came as near as anything to bursting into a roar of laughter.

Then he suddenly remembered supper and went off to prepare it.

The girl, left to herself, smiled. He had given her back that power and, like the sea elephants when they repulsed the penguins, he had given her something to smile over. She saw that he could not understand her in the least in a lot of little things, whilst she understood him through and through—or so she thought. She had thought the same about the sea elephants till the great battle, and—she had never seen Raft with murder in his eyes making the elements of beef tea.

He had made a stew for supper out of mussels, canned vegetables, seal meat and a piece of rabbit and when supper was over she went to bed in the bed he had made for her, for he had stripped the cache of all its wearing apparel and the remaining blankets, reserving the blankets for her use.

Then as she lay awake before dropping off to sleep she heard a sudden burst of noise from the night outside. It sounded as though one of the bulls had suddenly perceived a joke and were giving vent to his feelings.

She knew what it was, and she guessed the joke, and then, lying there in the dark, she began to laugh softly to herself with laughter that seemed to ease her mind of some old incubus clinging to it—less laughter than a sort of inverted form of crying and ending up almost in the latter with a few sniffs.

Then she fell asleep and dreamed that Raft had turned into something that seemed like a sea lion. She had never seen a sea lion, but this dream—one looked something like a lion and something like a sea elephant and something like Raft—with a touch of a carthorse. It had flippers, then it had wings, and the setting was the Place de la Concorde which bordered quite naturally the great beach of Kerguelen.

XXV

Stories on the Beach

For a week after that day not a word was said about their departure for that problematical bay to the westward where ships put in, or where they might put in should they find themselves in the region of Kerguelen. The idea seemed to the girl like one of those nightmare ideas, those terrific tasks which fever or indigestion sets to one in dreams.

It blew during that week as it had never blown before; blew from the north and the south and the west Atlantic oceans of rain driving seawards from the hills and passing off towards the islands, followed by breaks of clear weather and blue sparkling skies filled with the tearing screaming wind.

They talked a good deal during these days and at odd times, and the girl began to get some true glimpses of the mind of her companion, a mind that had never grown up, yet had in no wise deteriorated from remaining ungrown. Raft, who had been round the world a dozen times and more, knew less of the world than a modern child. Fights and roaring drunks and the smoke haze of bar rooms, wharf Messalinas and sailors' lodging houses had done him no harm at all. His innocence was vast and indestructible as his ignorance.

Bompard and La Touche were old men of the world compared to Raft; they were of different stuff, and being yachtsmen they had been long rubbed against the ways of high civilization.

To the girl, born and bred amongst all the intricacies of modern life and thought, and with a sense of mind-values as delicate as a jeweller's scales, Raft was a revelation.

She tried to sound his past. He had no past beyond the *Albatross*. He could tell all about the *Albatross* and his shipmates and the Old Man and so forth, but beyond that lay only a ship called the *Pathfinder*, and beyond that a muddle of ships and ports, a forest of masts stretching to a grey time an infinite distance away, the time of his childhood. He had no professed religion and he could neither read nor write.

Yet he had remembered her sou'wester, this man without a memory and he was always astonishing her by remembering little things she had said or things she had wished for.

HENRY DE VERE STACPOOLE

Of social distinction, beyond the division of afterguard from fo'c'sle, he seemed to possess little idea, save for a vague echo, caught from the man Harbutt, about the Rich People; and as to sex, beyond a queer instinctive delicacy and a tenderness due to her weakness and the memory of how he had found her, she might just as well have been a man, or a child like himself.

Another thing that struck her forcibly was the sense of his good humour. His mind seemed to possess an equable warm temperature, a temperature that it seemed impossible to lower or raise. She could not fancy him getting angry about anything. Had she seen him as in the past during one of his rare sprees, fighting the crowd and tossing men about like ninepins, she would have said: 'This is not the same man'— and maybe she would have been right.

"Where did you come from," said he one day to her as they sat rain-bound watching the gulls dashing about over the crests of the incoming seas.

"I came from Paris—you have never been to Paris?"

No, he had never been to Paris. He knew of the place, it was in France. Then she thought that she would interest him by trying to describe it. She spoke of the busy streets and the great Boulevards, then she tried to describe the people and what they were doing and then, as she talked, it was just as though Kerguelen had become the big end of a telescope and the doings of civilisation, as exemplified by Paris, a panorama seen at the little end.

What *were* they all doing, those crowds that she could visualize so plainly?—deputies, lawyers, military men, shop-keepers, pleasure seekers—towards what end were they going?

Then, with a strange little shock, it came to her that they were going, as a mass, nowhere except from dawn to dusk and dusk to dawn; that they were exactly like the crowd of sea gulls, each individual rotating in its own little orbit, and that the wonderful coloured and spangled crust called Civilization was nothing more than the excretion of individual ambitions, desires and energies.

Then, when she had finished her talk about the wonderful city of Paris, she found that Raft, comfortably propped against the cave wall, was asleep.

One of the disconcerting things about this huge creature was his capacity for sleep. He would drop asleep like a dog at the shortest notice and lie with his face in the crook of his arm like a dead man. She would watch him sometimes for half an hour together as he lay like this, and at first the vague fear used to come to her that he had been stricken by some malady in the form of sleeping sickness that made him act like this. She did not know that he had kept awake all those nights he had looked after her and that the same brain that could sleep and sleep and sleep could put sleep entirely away, just as the great body that lolled about like the sea elephants, could, like the sea-elephants, become a thing, tireless, and capable of infinite endurance.

Then again, he would smoke in silence for ages as though oblivious of her existence. She had observed the same thing in Bompard and La Touche who would sit cheek by jowl without a word, as though they had quarrelled. This trait pleased her, and she fell in with it unconsciously as though his mind had moulded hers and were teaching it the taciturnity of the sea.

One day, during a brief spell of calm when they were seated in the sun, dinner over and nothing to do, she tried the effect of literature upon him. She told him the story of Jack and the Bean Stalk and was delighted to find him interested when he had got his bearings and knew that a "giant" was a man fifty feet high; the cutting open of the giant—it occurred in her version—pleased him immensely. Then when she had finished she was alarmed to find, from words dropped by him, that he considered the story to be true, or at least to be taken seriously. She did not disillusion him; to do so she would have had to tell him that she had lied. That was the funny part of the thing. He would have said to himself "what made her lie to me about that chap?" By no possible means could he have imagined a person sitting down to invent in cold blood for the amusement of others a yarn about what never happened; no, it would have struck him as one of those lying personal yarns heard in the fo'c'sle sometimes and likely to produce a boot aimed at the teller's head. He had seen men reading books in the fo'c'sle occasionally and old newspapers, but of literature, fictional or otherwise, he had no more idea than the bull sea elephants of astronomy.

This she intuitively felt and so held her tongue. But she had interested him, and she went on, producing from her memory the story of the Forty Thieves.

Now he had accepted the bean stalk explanation, for he had never to his knowledge seen a bean stalk, but the jars in the Forty Thieves he revolted at, for a jar to him was a demijohn, or a thing of that size. A man could not get into that.

However, on explanation, he passed the jars, and the boiling oil repaid him. He seemed to delight in torture and blood.

"Where did you get that yarn from?" asked he.

"Out of a book," said she.

"Got anymore?" he asked.

"Plenty," she replied casting round in her mind, and wondering how it happens that children's stories run so frequently to blood and ferocity.

She remembered Anatole France's story of the juggler who juggled before the shrine of Our Lady, having no better offering to make to her, and Raft sat spellbound, after having made out that Our Lady was the Virgin Mary, the patron of Catholic shipmates. She told it so well and so simply, with unobtrusive foot notes as to monasteries and their contents, that he could not but see the point, the poor man having nothing to offer but his stock in trade of tricks, offered it.

Well, what of that? It was the best he had, and, if she could see the other chaps doing things for her, she could see him. The story, whose whole point lies in the supposed non-existence of the virgin as a discerning being, ought to cast its gentle ridicule not on the ignorant juggler but on the more learned brethren of the monastery. To Raft they were all in the same boat, and as to whether she could see them or not he didn't know.

The story fell flat, horribly flat, told to the absolutely simple hearted, and to the Teller, after explanations were over, it seemed that the Listener had in some way cut open modern genius and exposed a little tricky mechanism working on a view point of chilled steel.

That Raft, in fact, was so big in a formless way that he was much above the story.

She remedied her blunder on the next storytelling occasion with Blue Beard.

Then the weather broke fair and the islands drew away and the clouds rose high and the white terns, always flitting like dragon-flies amidst the other birds, rose like the clouds, they always flew higher in fine weather, and with the smooth seas a new thing shewed like a sign: the little sea elephants were no longer confining themselves to the river and near shore. Some of them were taking boldly to the sea. Their small heads could be seen sometimes quite a long way out.

This fact gave the girl food for thought. The summer was getting on.

It almost seemed that Ponting was right, that no ships would venture into that sea between the islands and the shore, and that their only hope of rescue lay in that bay away to the west, heaven knew how far.

Then an idea came to her. Two ships had already been here for certain: the wreck and the ship of Captain Slocum, then there was the cache, some ship must have left that.

She told Raft what was in her mind but got little consolation from him. He opined that the wreck wouldn't have been a wreck if she had kept clear of this dangerous water, that the cache might have been left by people who had landed somewhere else, and as for Captain Slocum's ship she might have been a whaler. Whalers according to Raft were always off the beaten track and poking their noses into places where honest deep sea ships would not dare to go.

"Well, then," said she, "how about that bay you spoke of?"

"Oh, that place," said Raft.

"Yes."

He hung silent for a moment as if revolving the question in his mind.

"But you were set against it," said he at last.

"Yes, I know, but I am stronger now, and it seems useless staying here till perhaps the winter comes."

She paused and looked towards the islands. She hated the idea of that journey which she pictured over rocks and across plains, where? In search of a place that might not exist, and where, if it did exist, no ship might perhaps be found. An almost hopeless journey involving unknown hardships.

"You ain't strong enough," suddenly said Raft.

It was as though he had touched some spring in her character that set the machinery of determination working.

"I am strong enough," she replied. Then after a moment's pause something in her began speaking, something that seemed allied to conscience, rather than thought, something that spoke almost against her will.

"We ought to go, we ought not to lose any chance. It seems almost hopeless, but it is the right thing to do. To stay here is not fighting, and in this place one has to fight if one wants to live or to get away. I feel that. To sit here with one's hands folded is wicked."

"Well, I believe in making a fight," said the other, "question is, will we be any the better."

"There's always the chance."

"Ay, there's always a chance."

Then an idea came to her.

"How about the boat?" she asked.

HENRY DE VERE STACPOOLE

"That old boat along the beach?"

"Yes, suppose we took her and rowed down the coast."

"There aren't no oars in her."

"There are oars. I hid them amongst the bushes and I can find them again."

Raft considered the proposition for a moment, then he shook his head and tapped the dottle out of his pipe.

"Not with them winds that get you here," said he, "they let out when you're least expecting it and we'd be on to the rocks and done for. I'm not saying if we had a boat crew we mightn't try, but we're underhanded. No, we'll have to hoof it if we go."

"Hoof it—what is that?" asked she.

"Walk it," replied Raft, "and I'm thinking it's beyond you, you aren't fit for travelling rough, like me."

"Aren't I?—I suppose I don't look strong, but I am, of course I'm not as strong as you, but I can keep on once I begin, and I have been through a good deal ever since that night we were wrecked, I don't think any journey we could make would be worse than that. And I was not prepared for all that as I am now for anything that may happen. Think of it, we had all been sitting at dinner, it was only a little while after dinner and I had my evening frock on."

"Your evening which?"

"Dress. They were all rich people on board the yacht and they put on different clothes always for dinner. It seems stupid—well, I was down below and I suddenly felt that I must get on deck, so I put on these clothes and my oilskin and sou'wester, then, as I was coming upstairs the collision happened. I got on deck and it was quite dark until the electric light was put on, then I saw the stern of your ship with the name on it."

She paused with a little shudder and seemed visualizing the terrible picture again.

"Heave ahead," said Raft interestedly.

"Then I was thrown into a boat and forgot everything until I woke in the early morning alone with those two men. It was all just like that. I wasn't prepared for hardship as I am now, and I hadn't a companion like you. Those two men were no use."

"How's that?" asked he.

"Well, they were always grumbling."

"Swabs."

"I didn't mind that so much, but they were no use, they wouldn't do things. I had to make them go and hunt for firewood, they might just as well have had no hands. Bompard, the oldest one wasn't so bad—"

"It was the other chap you done in," said Raft. "Well, I reckon you've been through it. Rum thing I saw you first when I was handling a topsail in that blow. The weather broke and I was holdin' on to the yard when I sighted you away to starboard with the sun on you. Old Ponting was close to me and he yelled out he'd seen you before and give you your name, the *Gaston de Paree*."

"And we sighted you," said she, "I was down below when the steward came with a message that there was a ship in sight, I came up and there you were with the sun on you and the storm clouds behind, and do you know you frightened me."

"How so?" asked Raft.

"I don't know. I felt there was going to be a disaster of some sort—it was almost like a warning."

"Well, there's no saying," said Raft. "I've known a chap warned he was going to be drowned, and drowned he was sure enough. I was down below asleep and shot out of my bunk by the smash; then I was on the main deck, the chaps all round shouting for boats, and if you ask me how I got off I couldn't tell you. One minute a big light was blazing, then it was black as thunder. My mind seemed to go when the black came on, I'd no more thought than a blind puppy. Something saved me. That's all I know."

"God saved you," said the girl.

"Well, maybe He did," said Raft; "but what made Him let all the other chaps drown?"

"I don't know," she replied, "but He saved you just as He saved me. I know He looks after things. Look at those sea elephants and the gulls; He leads them about by instinct."

"What's that?" asked Raft.

"Instinct," said she, suddenly formulating the idea, "is God's mind, it tells the birds and elephants where to get food and where to go and how to avoid danger; you and I have minds of our own, but our minds are nothing to the minds of the birds and animals. They are never wrong. Look out there at those porpoises."

"Them black fish," said Raft, shading his eyes.

"Yes, well, look at the way they are going along, they are on a journey, going somewhere, led by instinct, and I think when human beings find

HENRY DE VERE STACPOOLE

themselves having to fight for life they fall back on instinct, the mind of God comes to help them. Look at me. I believe I found that cache led by instinct and I would never have pulled through only instinct told me I would, somehow. God's mind told me."

"Well, there's no saying," said Raft.

"I don't want to leave here," she went on, "but I feel we ought to go. The chances seem small, even if we find that bay; still, I feel we ought to go."

"I'm feelin' the same way myself," said Raft.

"Then we will go and the sooner we start the better."

"I'm thinking of them porpoises," said Raft.

"What about them?"

"Well, there's a saying they hug the shore pretty close if bad weather is coming. It's fine today, but I've a feeling there's going to be another blow soon and maybe we'd better wait till it's over—maybe it's instinc'," he finished, looking round shyly.

The girl laughed. "If you feel like that," said she, "we had certainly better wait. Maybe the porpoises were sent to tell us."

"There's no saying," replied he. They were seated on the rocks just where she had watched the great battle and far and near the "sea cows" were sunning themselves on the rocks whilst beyond the seal beach the penguins were drilling in long lines. Scarcely a breath of wind stirred and the sea lay calm like a sheet of dim blue glass to where the islands sat beneath the sky of summer.

But the islands had drawn closer since morning and the birds seemed busier than usual and more clamorous. To the eastward where the cliffs rose higher, guillemots had their home on the ledges of basalt and the wheezy bagpipe-like cry of them came in bursts every now and then as though they were angry about something, whilst the cry of the razorbills and the "get-away, get-away" of the kittiwakes had a sharper note. The puffins alone were calm, swimming in coveys on the glassy water and leaving long ripples in their wake.

XXVI

The Great Wind

The sun sank, broadened out and banded with mist beyond the Lizard Point, and before his upper limb had been swallowed by the rocks the business began with a blow from the hills.

Most winds come in gusts and pauses, this wind from the Infernal Regions came at first steady and warm, never ceasing, steadily growing like the thrust of an infinite sword driven with a rapidly increasing momentum and a murmur like the voice of Speed herself.

Raft and the girl saw that the sea elephants were herding up into the shelter of the cliffs and that the gulls had vanished as though they had never been.

And still the wind increased, its voice now a long monotonous cry, steadily sharpening, yet deepening, stern as the Voice of Wrath.

"It's blowing up," said Raft, "and there's more coming."

Then over the cliff and undershot by the last rays of sunset came the clouds chased and harried by the wind, tearing before and torn by the teeth of the gale.

Raft and the girl stood watching till pebbles and rocks the size of coconuts began to fall on the beach blown over the cliff edge, till the sea, flat and milk-white, seemed to bend under the stress, till it would seem that the very islands would be blown away.

The girl felt light-headed and giddy as though the rush above had rarefied the air under the cliffs. Not a drop of rain fell, the wind held the sky and the whole world. It seemed loosed from some mysterious keeping never to be recaptured until it had blown the sea away and flattened the earth.

And still it increased.

Raft, taking the girl by the arm, drew her back into the cave; she was trembling. It seemed to her that this was no storm, that something had gone wrong with the scheme of things, that this Voice steadily being keyed up was the voice of some string keeping everything together, stretched to its utmost and sure to snap.

Then it snapped.

The whole of Kerguelen seemed to burst like a bomb-shell with a blaze of light shewing islands and sea.

Then again it seemed to burst with a light struggling through a deluge.

The boom of the rain on the sea came between the thunder crashes whilst a giant on the hills seemed to stand steadily working a flashlight, a light so intense that now and again through broken walls of rain the islands could be seen like far white ghosts wreathed in mist.

They sat down on the floor of the cave and the man put his arm about the girl as if to protect her; then something came sniffing at them, it was a little sea elephant that had got astray and scared by the work outside had crept in for shelter and company. The girl rested her hand on it and it lay still.

It seemed to her now that she could hear the gods of the storm as they battled, hear their cries and breathing and trampling, whilst every moment a thousand foot giant in full armour would come crashing to earth, knee, shoulder and helmet hitting the rocks in succession.

"It's a big blow," came Raft's voice, "no call to be scared."

He was holding her to him like a child whilst she held to her the little sea elephant, and so they remained, the three of them until the big blow, failing to tear Kerguelen from its foundations, began to pause like a spent madman.

The flashlight man on the hills began to work his apparatus more slowly and now the thunder seemed doing its vast work away out at sea and all sounds became gradually merged in the enormous, continuous sound of the rain.

The little sea elephant seemed suddenly to take fright at the strange company it found itself in and went tumbling and sniffing out to find its mates, whilst through the night came the occasional "woof" of a bull as if giving praise that the worst was over.

"The old sea cows know it's done," said Raft, "now you'd better get under your blankets,—you aren't afraid to be alone?"

"I'm not afraid a bit now," said she. She patted his hand as a child might and he crawled out and she heard him swearing at the rain as he made for his hole in the cliff.

She remembered the porpoises and fell to thinking of what would have happened had she and Raft started on their expedition yesterday or the day before. That wind, which sent rocks flying on to the beach, would have blown them away.

She said this next morning as they stood watching the sea. The sea was worth watching. The due-south wind had stirred the heart of the ocean from west of Enderby land, and, like a trumpeter, was leading a vast flood that split on Heard Island only to re-form and burst on the southern shores of Kerguelen.

They could hear the vague far-off roar of it all those leagues away beyond the mountains, mixed with the cry of the wind still blowing a full gale, and beyond the shelter of the land they could see the islands getting it, bombarded by the waves and up to their shoulders in sea-smoke and foam.

Then as they stood, suddenly and like a thing shot dead, the wind ceased, and in the silence the roar of the beaches far and near arose like a fume of sound. Then, as suddenly, the wind came shouting out of the west, piling up a cross sea that leapt like the water in a boiling pot.

"I'm thinking when this blow is over we may have a spell of fine weather," said Raft, "and it will be just as well for us to be making our plans and getting things ready so's we won't be behind hand when the fine spell comes."

"I think so too," said she, "we will have to take food with us—how much?"

"Enough for a month," said he, "who knows, we may have to come back, and there's not much to be had elsewhere." Then he fell into thought for a moment, "maybe stuff for a fortnight will be enough for there's birds and rabbits to be got, and gulls' eggs. Them old penguins let you screw their necks as if it come natural to them, we don't want to take too big a load."

Then they found themselves at a loss, it was quite easy to arrange to take a fortnight's food, but how much did that mean?

They determined to use two blankets for sacks and then made a rough calculation, based on imagination, and collected together tins of meat and vegetables and the remaining biscuits, the result was a burden that two people might have carried but not very far.

"We've overshot it," said Raft.

"We'll never be able to carry all that," said the girl, "or if we did we would have to go so slowly that the journey would be much longer—it cuts both ways."

They reduced the load by nearly a half.

"There's one thing," said he, "there's no call to take water with us, there's holes full of water everywhere, seems to me in this place."

Then he turned to look at the weather.

The wind was less and the clouds were thinning and the air had the feel of a break coming. Then, just before sunset the clouds parted in the west and the sun went down in a sky red as blood.

"We'll start tomorrow," said Raft.

PART V

XXVII

The Corridor

The next morning broke grey and fair.

When the girl came out she found that Raft had collected the things to be taken in one bundle tied up in a blanket. He had also set out breakfast. The remainder of the stores he had stacked at the back of the cave where he slept.

These stores, with what was still in the cache, would be useful if they had to come back to the beach.

"But what am I to carry?" asked she.

"Oh, there's no call for you to trouble," answered he, "you've got your oilskins. I reckon that'll be enough for you to bother with. Them things in the bundle is no weight for a man."

She tried to argue the question. It seemed to her impossible that any single person could carry that load for long, but she might just as well have argued with the gentle wind blowing now shorewards from the islands. He lifted the bundle with one great hand to demonstrate its lightness; he was also going to take the harpoon as a sort of walking stick.

It seemed to her that she had never realized his strength before, nor his placid determination that seemed more like an elemental force than the will of a man.

She gave in and sat down to the meal, biscuits and the remains of a stew, and as she ate she watched the great sea bulls and the cows and the young ones that now were able to land, boosting through the foam like their elders, and as she watched she wondered whether she would ever see these things again, there, against the setting of the sea and the great islands.

She had put on her boots for the journey and a pair of men's soft woollen socks from the store in the cache. They were small men's socks and the wool was so fine and soft that the size did not trouble her. In her pocket she still carried the few odds and ends including the tobacco box in which she had placed her rings. She wore the sou'wester, and the oilskin lay beside her folded and ready to be carried on her arm.

Then, when the meal was finished, Raft washed the plates and stored them in the cave. He stood looking at the stored things for a moment as if to make sure they would be all right, then he kicked an old tin away into a cleft of the rocks as though to tidy the place, then he took up the harpoon and slung the bundle on his shoulder.

The girl rose and looked around her. This place where she had suffered and nearly died was still warm with memories, and the sea creatures were like friends, she had grown to love them just as people love trees or familiar inanimate things.

To associate the idea of home with that desolate beach, those moving monsters, those caves, would seem absurd. Well, it was like leaving home, and as she stood looking around her a tightness came in her throat and her eyes grew misty. But Raft was moving now and she followed him, glancing back now and then until they crossed the river where she looked back for the last time. The river was almost deserted now by the young sea elephants, except at its mouth. A few little girl seals lay about, delicate or unadventurous creatures whose lives would doubtless be short in a world that is only for the strong. These little girl seals had attracted her attention before, they had almost the ways of fine ladies. It was as though some germ of civilization in the herd had become concentrated in them and she had wondered whether they would ever pull through the rough and tumble of life, recognising vaguely that nature is opposed to civilization at heart. They seemed allied to herself and their future seemed as doubtful as her own here where nothing helped, where everything opposed.

She caressed them with her eyes for the last time; then as she turned and followed Raft she forgot them. Her brave mind, that nothing could daunt but loneliness, faced the great adventure ahead not only undaunted but uplifted. The way was terrific, the chances were small, so small, so remote, that they could scarcely be called chances, and the penalty of failure was return and a winter here when the beach would be deserted by all but the gulls. The very desperation of the business made it great, and from the greatness came the uplift.

They passed the figure-head with its sphinx-like face staring over the sea, and the great skull half sanded over by the recent blow. Then they drew near the caves and the boat.

The boat had been blown over on its other side by the wind and lay with one gunnel deep buried in the sand and its keel presented to the cliffs; she glanced only once at the caves, deserted now by the birds who had no doubt picked the last fragments of the dead man.

Then they climbed the Lizard rocks and at the highest point sat down to rest for a moment.

Raft, with the bundle beside him and the harpoon held between his knees, swung his head from the great beach on his right to the broken country on his left.

He said nothing, not wishing perhaps to dishearten his companion. It was she who spoke.

"That's the plain I told you of," said she, "we mustn't cross it, you can see from here some of the dangerous patches, those yellow ones, but there are others just as bad that you can't tell till you are trapped in them. I would have gone down, only a bird flying overhead dropped a fish on the ground right in front of me and the fish disappeared."

"We'd better get along the sea-shore rocks, seems to me," said Raft, "the tide's going out, all them rocks between tide marks is pretty flat."

"Suppose the tide comes in," said she, "and we can't get up the cliffs?"

"Oh, we'll have lots of time to make a good way before it comes back," replied he, "and we've got to trust a bit to chance, we've got to strike bold. I reckon we'd better trust to instinc'." He laughed in his beard. "The same sort of instinc' that made that bird drop the fish to give you soundin's of that mud hole."

"Providence," said she, "yes—you are right."

"I believe in strikin' bold," said he, almost as though he were talking to himself. "It's like fighting with a chap, the fellow that does the hittin' without bothering about bein' hit. He's the chap. Well, if you're restored, we'll be gettin' along."

He heaved up and led the way, striking right down to the sea and pausing now and then to help her. Once he lifted her as though she were a feather from one rock to the other. Then, all of a sudden they came to a ten foot drop. There was no getting round that drop, it was a basalt step that circled the whole Lizard Point on its seaward side. It did not disconcert Raft. He threw the harpoon down, then he lowered himself, clutching the edge and let himself fall. Following his directions she threw him the bundle. It would have felled an ordinary landsman, but he caught it, placed it beside him and then ordered her to jump, just as she stood, without lowering herself.

"Jump with your arms up," said he, laughing, "no call to lower yourself. I'll catch you."

It was like an order to commit suicide. It seemed to her impossible, she thought that he only spoke in fun, then she knew that he was in earnest, that he was ordering her. But it was impossible—absolutely. Then she jumped with arms raised, jumped into two great hands that clipped her round the waist and brought her, feet to ground, with scarcely a jar.

"I didn't think you'd have done it," said he. "You ain't wanting in pluck."

"I knew it would be all right if you told me," said she, "but I didn't want to do it until the very last moment."

After that she would have jumped over a cliff if he had told her. It seemed to her that he was invincible—infallible.

A climb of a couple of minutes brought them down to the tide mark rocks, the tide was a quarter out and the sea comparatively calm and the rocks flat-topped like those of the seal beach and free from seaweed except where, here and there, were piled masses of giant kelp torn up from its deep sea attachments and cast here by the waves. It lay in ridges that had to be climbed over sometimes and seemed entirely confined to the Lizard Point and the rocks beyond, for when they reached where the cliffs began it ceased to occur.

Where the cliffs began they first experienced the true meaning of a journey along that coast.

She had seen these cliffs from the boat, but that view, though forbidding enough, had told her little of the reality.

They rose from two to four hundred feet in height, these cliffs, and looking up was like looking up a wall of polished ebony.

Here and there they were streaked with long lines of white where the guillemots in their thousands sat on ledges, and here and there they were faced by seaward rocks standing out in the water and carved by the waves into all sorts of fantastic shapes, but waves and rocks and sea and sky, all these were nothing, here the cliffs were everything, dominating the mind and soul, sinister, and tinging every sound from the wave echoes to the gull voices with tragedy.

And high tide mark was the cliff base in fine weather, in foul, the waves would lash and dash and beat fifty feet up, there was not a guillemot ledge lower than eighty feet, puffins, razorbills and kittiwakes, who always build above the guillemots did not seem to come here at all, keeping to the seaward rocks and the coast line where the cliffs drew further away from the sea.

With the sea so close on the right and the cliffs on the left the girl felt like a mouse in a trap designed for an elephant. Alone she would never have dared this road, even with Raft leading her she felt timid and oppressed. The place did not seem to affect Raft. Plodding ahead as indifferently as though he were on some civilized country road, he talked to her now and then over his shoulder, calling attention to queer shaped crabs or dead kelp fish, and ever as they went their road grew broader as the tide drew out.

It was now about an hour and a half after high water, that is to say, quarter ebb; in a little more than ten hours it would be high water again, before that they must find a way from the beach or be drowned. Raft knew this and the girl knew it too. It seemed almost impossible that, with so much time before them, they could not find a break in the cliffs towards safe ground, yet the cliffs seemed to stretch endlessly before them and their pace was slow, not more than three miles an hour. They rested sometimes for a moment watching the out-going sea and the gulls; unused to exercise the girl was tired, and the man knew it. Alone he could have travelled swiftly and without resting, but he said nothing, and though he knew the necessity of speed, it was he who made the halts for the sake of his companion. Three hours after noon he took some food out of the bundle and made her eat. They had already drunk from a little torrent rushing out of a crack in the cliff wall, but even so the food seemed dry and she could scarcely swallow it. Anxiety had her in its grip, the cliffs stretching on and on interminably seemed like misfortune itself made visible.

Said Raft: "The tide's near the turn and them cliffs don't shew no sign of a cut in them, but then there's only two miles or so to be seen from here. Round that bend there's no knowing, they may break away beyond there. What I'm thinkin' is this. We've time to get back along the road we've come by before it's high water again."

"Go back?"

"We've time to do it; if we keep on our course it will take us maybe near an hour to get to that shoulder and from there we won't have much time to get back before high water again. We've cut it too fine and if the tide comes back and catches us before we get to a break we're done."

She looked forward then she looked back. They were in a veritable corridor. The sea formed the right hand wall of this corridor, the cliffs varying from two hundred to three hundred feet high formed the left hand wall, cliffs black as ebony, polished by sea washing, unclimbable and tremendous as a dream of Dante.

She saw their full position. There was time to get back from where they stood, but if they went on to the cape of cliff before them there would be no time to get back, they would have to go on, and the unseen cliffs beyond that cape might stretch for twenty miles unclimbable as here.

Yet the idea of going back was horrible, heartbreaking.

She saw that Raft was between two moods. Then she said to him.

"If you were alone would you go back or go on?"

"Me?" said Raft. He paused for a moment as if in thought—"Oh, I reckon I'd go on."

"Then we will go on."

"I was thinkin' of you," said he.

"I know—but I could not bear to go back. If we fail now like that we will fail altogether. Imagine going all that way back. No, I couldn't. We must risk it."

"I'm thinking that way," said he.

He picked up the bundle and harpoon and they started, and no sooner had she taken the first step than Fear laid his hand on her heart and a wild craving to return seized her so that she could have cried out.

She had once said that she feared an ugly face more than a blow, and the fear that seized her now was less the fear of death than the fear of the cliffs and their conspiracy with the murmuring sea that would soon be an inclosing wall.

She fought it down.

The cliff shoulder was further away than they thought; it took them an hour to reach it and, when they turned it, there, before them lay cliffs higher, more monstrous and running in a curve to another shoulder seven miles away, if a yard. But towards the middle of the curve the cliff face seemed ridged and broken near the base. Raft shading his eyes, pointed out this broken surface.

"It looks as if there was foothold there beyond tide mark," said he, "we've got to go on anyhow—Lord, but you're tired!"

He made her sit down. The sight of that gargantuan sweep of cliff coming on top of the weariness of the journey had crushed her. To go forward seemed impossible, to fight against that immensity impossible. She could have wept but she had neither tears nor energy. The gods seemed to have built those bastions to shut out all hope and the voice of the returning sea seemed like a tide turning over her broken thoughts like pebbles.

Raft standing over her like a tower said not a word.

Mixed with the voice of the sea came the voices of the gulls and all sorts of sea echoes from the cliffs.

Then as she sat she made a supreme effort of mind. She must rise and go on. She struggled to rise, but her limbs had left her, deserted her, stricken as if by paralysis.

Raft took off his cap and put it in his pocket, then he went to the cliff side and rested the harpoon against it, standing up. She watched him, vaguely wondering what he was about, then he returned to her and bent down and she found herself lifted suddenly and seated on his left shoulder.

"Hold on to my hair," cried he. Then he bent and picked up the bundle, went to the cliff side and picked up the harpoon and started. The giant strength that had caught her when she jumped from the Lizard Point ledge was carrying her now like a feather, the crook of his left arm round her legs to steady her, the harpoon clutched in his left hand, the bundle swung over his right shoulder.

And she held on to his hair as a child might, without a word, and as she held the strength of him seemed to permeate her through her fingers casting fear and misery out.

She felt as a tiny tired child feels when caught up and carried by its mother, and carrying her so he strode on, cursing himself for not having carried her before.

It was a three-mile journey to that roughness on the cliff and as he drew near he saw that they were saved, at least for the time.

The rock broke here in ledges like steps and twenty feet up and well beyond tide mark ran a little plateau some ten or twelve feet broad.

She saw it as well as he and filled with new strength she cried out to be set down.

"Stay easy," said Raft. "It's easier to carry the bundle with you on my shoulder, you ain't no weight."

Then when he reached the steps:

"Done it b'God," said he.

He dropped the bundle and harpoon, and, lifting her, set her feet on the basalt steps.

"Can you climb it?" asked he.

Without a word she climbed and sitting on the little plateau looked down on him.

Then he followed with the things and took his seat beside her. They sat for a while without a word, the bare rocks and the grey sea before them.

A great rock out at sea, pierced and arched like the frame work of a door, shewed through its opening the sea beyond. Gulls flew round it and their eternal complaint came on the wind blowing, still lightly, from the north.

Raft seemed absorbed in thought.

Then he said: "It won't be high water until gettin' on for dark. We'd better stick here the night anyhow and get the low tide tomorrow. But there's time for me now to get to that next shoulder and see what's beyond, it's a matter of four miles there maybe and four miles back."

"I'll go with you," said she, "I'm stronger now."

"No, you stick here," said he. "There's no call for two to go. You'll want your strength for the morning."

"Only for you I wouldn't be here," said she.

"Well, maybe you wouldn't," said Raft. "It's as well I was along with you, but you ain't no weight—no more than a kitten. I never thought you were as bad as that or I'd have lifted you miles back."

"Aren't you tired?" she asked.

"Me—oh, no, not more than a bit stiff in the arm." He stretched his left arm out. Then he looked at the bundle.

"You don't want nothing to eat just yet?" asked he.

"Not till you come back," she answered. "I'll watch you from here."

He scrambled down, picked up the harpoon which he had left on the rocks and then looked up and nodded to her.

"I'll keep in sight," said he. Then he started.

She watched his great figure as it went, harpoon in hand, growing smaller and smaller, till, now, she could have covered it with her thumb nail. As the distance increased it seemed to go slower and the great black cliffs to grow higher.

At a dizzy height above her cormorants had their nests, they seemed angry about something as they clanged and flew, shooting out into the sky and wheeling back again in an aimless manner. Before her the grey sea crawled, coming, now, steadily shoreward.

The tide seemed coming in faster than usual. She knew that this could not be so and that Raft was too wise to allow himself to be cut off, all the same a smouldering anxiety fed on her heart as she watched the tiny figure now approaching the out-jutting shoulder of cliff. Then it disappeared.

He had promised to keep in sight.

Evidently that was impossible if he wanted to get a view of what lay beyond.

A minute passed, two, three—then the figure reappeared and her heart that had lain still sprang to life again.

As he drew closer she saw him stoop and pick up something, then he came right up to the cliff face, paused a minute and continued his way towards her, walking more slowly now and carrying the thing in his hands.

It was a big shell shaped like an abalone. He had filled it with water from a little torrent running from the cliff and when he reached her he held it up to show.

"We're all right," cried he, "there's only four or five miles of cliff beyond the point, then it breaks away down to the beach. We'll be able to get clear of this tomorrow."

She came down the basalt steps and took the shell from him. He had washed it in the torrent so that the water had no taint of salt. Then, carrying it carefully she got it to the plateau where he followed her.

XXVIII

Night

Towards dark the incoming tide began to hit the cliff base. Raft had taken the things from the bundle and had made her wrap herself in the blanket. "You ain't used to the weather like me," said he, "and this is nothing to bother about. Lucky it's not blowing. Lucky we made this shelf. Hark at that!"

The first full blow of a wave hit the basalt below them with a heart-sickening thud; then miles of stricken cliff began to boom. The terrific corridor was no more, and between them and the Lizard point so many miles away to the east and the point of safety miles away to the west, there was nothing but cliff washed by sea.

"A rotten coast," said Raft as they listened. "Only for this shelf we'd be down there."

"We'd have been flung against the cliff and beaten to pieces," said she.

"That's so," said Raft.

"When we get free from this," she said, "let us keep inland. I don't mind climbing over rocks, anything is better than the coast, under these cliffs."

"We've got to keep pretty close to the cliffs, all the same, to strike that bay," he replied, "hope it's there."

"It is there," said she. "I feel—I know it is there and that we will find a ship. We are being looked after."

"Which way?"

"We are being led. You remember when you saved me from dying in that cave, well, you were making for the bay then. If you had not found me you would have kept on and you would have crossed that plain where the bog places are, it looked the easiest way."

"That's so," said Raft.

"Bompard was swallowed up there. You would have been swallowed up too; you were led to find me for both our sakes. Then, today, I could have gone no further only for you, and you remember how we thought of going back? This ledge was here waiting for us. It tells us we have to go on and be brave and everything will come right."

"Well, maybe, you aren't far wrong," replied the other, "we've scraped through so far and maybe we'll scrape through to the end. My main wish is to have a plank under foot again, there ain't no give and take in land, I'm never surefooted on land, there's no lift in it. I reckon I'm like one of them sea chickens not used to solid stuff underfoot. D'you know what one of them gulls does first thing he lands on board a ship by chance?"

"No."

"He gets sick as a dog."

The cliff had an echo which, when it was not answering some loud boost of the sea managed to return words, and between the smack of two waves the girl heard it remark something about a dog. But the echo of the cliff soon had its mouth too full to hold words. The sea now nearly at full flood was bringing big waves along with it. In the gloom they could see the racing grey ghosts, and here, on account of the curve, there was little rhythm in the sound of it that came like the continuous thunder of big drums. At their feet, like the licking vicious tongue of the roaring monster, came the continuous gash-gash of waves washing up and falling back.

The girl sat with the blanket around her leaning close up against the man. She felt as a person feels standing before the cage of a tiger uncertain as to the strength of the bars, sometimes a puff of wind brought a touch of spray on her face, whilst the continuous muffled thunder of the coast leagues seemed like the bastions of the whole world at war with the sea.

"There's no call to be afraid," said Raft. He seemed, by some special faculty, to be able to divine her feelings.

"I'm not exactly afraid," she replied. "It's just that everything seems so big—and those cliffs, now, even when they are hidden, they make one know they are there, they seem wicked and alive, yet not able to move."

"You've hit it," said he, "they're for all the world as if they were looking at a chap. It's a rotten coast, but it's near high water now and the tide will soon be drawing out."

This cheered her.

Then the whale birds began to cry and flit about. The whale birds are blind by daylight and their voices scarcely ever heard, they are the owls of the sea.

The girl talked about them for something to say, then she fell to wondering why on a beach like this there were no sea elephants. Raft explained "sea cows" would never come to a washed beach like this, there were no dry rocks for them to "hang about" on.

He had lit his pipe with the tinder box and the smell of the tobacco came good and comforting, the slap and dash of the waves sounded less vicious, too, as though the sea had done its worst to get at them and was foiled.

Then she said, apropos of nothing but the last of her wandering thoughts: "Have you ever seen a man killed?"

He laughed as though over some pleasant reminiscence. "Dozens." Then he began to recall chaps he had seen killed, falling from aloft and otherwise. He had seen one hit the sea such a smack it split him open, and he had seen a chap under water being pulled to pieces by sharks just as terriers pull an old shoe.

Then he wandered off to a bar scene where a dago—it was at Nagasaki—had been drinking rice rum and knifed a man, a regular prosy old sailor's yarn, with "I says to him," and "he says to me" at every turn.

Then he found that she was leaning more heavily against him and was asleep. He put his pipe beside him and slipped an arm round her. Then, as though sleep were infectious, down he sank still holding her and there they lay. He snoring gently and she with her head pillowed on his chest.

XXIX

The Summit

I will break thee." Across Kerguelen those words are written to be read by the soul of man. The rock, the rain, the wind and the sea, these, as instruments, would surely be sufficient for the carrying out of the threat; but the soul of man is strong, hence the spirit of Kerguelen has called to its assistance Fog.

Since landing on the great beach the girl had seen the islands fog-wreathed several times but the beach itself had only once been attacked.

When she awoke on the rock plateau the first word of Raft to her was "fog."

They had slept as the dead sleep for nine hours and Raft had awoken with the girl's head still on his chest and feeling as though he were packed in damp cotton wool. It was after sun up and the fog was so dense that the edge of the plateau was only just visible. Through the fog came the breaking of the waves; the tide was coming in again.

Raft had lit his pipe and the girl, stiff from lying, rose up and stamped about to warm herself. Neither of them spoke a word in the way of grumbling.

The plateau was about twenty yards in length and by drawing off five yards or so one could have a dressing-room screened with a fog veil, so the fog was not an unmixed evil.

Then they breakfasted, listening to the slashing of the water just below and counting the time till the out-going sea would let them loose.

"It's a good job I went to the point last night," said Raft, "else we wouldn't be able to start in this smother, not knowing what was beyond there."

"Will we be able to start in this?" she asked.

"Lord, yes," replied he, "the cliffs will give us a lead, it'll be slow going but we'll do it all right, it's not more than six miles or so to the break from the point there."

"When can we start?"

Raft listened to the water below, it was breaking now against the near rocks but not yet against the cliff base.

"In another three hours or maybe a bit more," said he.

An hour later, as though the Fog spirit had been listening and watching, and as though it despaired of its attack on the heart of the prisoners, the smother began to thin; by the time the tide reluctantly began to free them it had broken up and patches of the blessed blue sky shewed overhead.

By the time they reached the point and had a view of the great cliff break-down that would give them release it was fine weather, with a gently heaving sea breaking in beneath a sky of summer.

It was as though their troubles were ended. At noon they reached the great break-down and a new form of country.

Stretching inland almost to the foothills lay a broad valley, boulder strewn, and looking like the bed of some vanished river. Before them to the west the ground rose from the valley, gently, unbroken, desolate, like nothing so much as the desolate country that borders the Riff coast of Morocco. But it was ease itself compared to the tumble of rocks around and beyond the Lizard Point.

Down the middle of the valley came a little wimpling rivulet like the remains of the river that had once been. They drank from it and rested and had some food, then they started with light hearts, taking the easy ascent to the high ground, treading a moss dark and springy like the moss that covers the old lava beds of Iceland.

"Look!" said the girl.

They had reached the highest point and before them, away to the west, stretched the same rolling dark-smooth country, making low cliffs at the sea edge and then, as if weary of little things, springing gigantic and bold towards the sky.

"It's over there the bay would be," said Raft. "Ponting said it was a black brute of a bay between two cliffs rising higher than a ship's top masts. Well, there's our chance before us—if you call it a chance. It's a long way, taking it how you will."

Chance! Despite her optimism and belief in being led, as she stood now with the wind blowing in her face it seemed to her that she stood before absolute hopelessness.

Nothing, not even the sea corridor, had balked her like that terrible distance, calm, sunlit, yet gloomy like a recumbent giant.

The monstrosity of the whole adventure unmasked itself of a sudden; travelling to find a bay they had heard of on the chance of finding a ship—a ship on a coast where ships were scarcely to be found.

And even if they found the bay they could not wait for a ship. Here

HENRY DE VERE STACPOOLE

there was no food, with the exception of rabbits and gulls. The ship would have to be there, waiting for them.

Raft must have been mad! mad! mad! She herself must have been mad to dream of such a thing.

Her lips felt dry as pumice stone and she glanced at her companion as he stood with the bundle at his feet and the harpoon in his hand, looking about him, far and near, as unconcerned as though beyond that great hump on the skyline lay a sure town with a railway station.

No, Raft was not mad. He was unconcerned. He knew, even better than she, the hopelessness of their position, yet he was calm and unmoved, never from the first moment she had seen him had he been otherwise; before everything, like a rock, he continued.

Yet it was only now, as he quietly stood there surveying their "chance," that he came home to her truly as he was, unbreakable; simple, vast, forged by the sea. She swallowed down the devil of doubt and despair as she stood looking at him standing so, and she was about to speak when, catching sight of something along the high ground to the right he pointed it out to her. She saw a white point on the ground a couple of hundred yards away.

As they drew close to it it enlarged and other things shewed. It was the top of a skull belonging to a skeleton tucked away in a little hollow as though it were sheltering from the wind.

Rags of clothing still hung to it and the boots were there still that had once belonged to it.

"Wonder what did that poor chap in?" said Raft as he stood looking at it. "Wrecked, most likely and lost himself—well, it's a sign folk have been here, anyhow."

He gauged the measure of the desolation around by his words. Here a skeleton did not make the desolation more desolate; on the contrary, it proved that folk had been here.

So the girl felt.

"He'd have been blown away by this only for that hollow he's in," said Raft, "well, he's out of his troubles whoever he was and whatever ship he hailed from."

"We can't bury him," said she.

"He's buried," said Raft.

He had summed up Kerguelen in two words and there was almost a trace of bitterness in his voice. Beyond the remark that it was a brute of a coast he had never grumbled against the place or abused it or the Almighty for making it, as many a man has done; and now at the summit of things two words sufficed him.

Then, leaving the skeleton to the wind and the sky and the countless ages, they turned and went on their way west.

XXX

THE BAY

It took them till dusk to reach the foot of the western rise of ground; here they slept under a rock, continuing their way next morning, climbing till they reached the summit of the rise and keeping their course along the edge of a cliff that fell a sheer three hundred feet to the shore below.

Sometimes Raft peeped over the cliff edge and once the girl drew close and looked, too, dizzy with the height, made more dreadful by the gulls flying far below.

At noon, far ahead of them, they saw something that made them pause; a little mound. As they drew closer they knew. It was another cache, a cache made of heaped earth and loose stones with about a foot of sign post protruding from it. The post had been broken off in some storm and blown away.

"There'll be stuff under there," said Raft, "and if we have to go back it'll come in handy. It's a pointer to the bay anyhow; there must be some landin' place near here, we've only got to keep on."

They sat down and rested and had some food, eating as much as they wanted now that they had a store to depend on. They had drunk twice that morning from pot holes still half-filled with the rain of a few days ago and they had no need of water—it is the one thing a man never needs in Kerguelen. They were in good spirits; the haunting fear that their provisions might not be enough to last them for the return journey was gone; also, if the bay were near, they could remain now sometime, even take up their quarters here to wait on the chance of a ship.

The idea came to them to make a burrow into the cache, now, working with the harpoon and their hands, and for the purpose of verifying the contents; but they put it away, the desire to get on drove them like a whip and they went on, halting towards dusk and sleeping in a hollow that gave them shelter from the wind that was blowing from the south.

Towards dawn the wind changed to the west and at the first rays of light Raft awoke, sat up and sniffed. Then he laid his hand on the girl's shoulder.

"Smell that!" cried he.

She sat up, her eyes half-blind with sleep.

"Smell the wind!" said Raft.

She turned her face to the west. On the wind was coming the ghost of a smell, faint and horrible and soul-searching.

"That's a ship," said Raft.

"A ship!"

"Boiling down blubber. I struck that smell once, seven years ago; it's blubber. I reckon we're all right." He heaved himself on to his feet and the girl half-rose, kneeling, and looked at him.

"Are you sure?"

"Sure as sure; smell it."

Then, as she sniffed again, she knew. That was not a nature smell; horrible though it was it was not the tragic smell of corruption. It had something, almost one might say, low down about it, little, mean, business-like—it was her first sniff of returning Civilization, the first impression on an olfactory sense cleared and cleaned by the winds of Kerguelen.

She looked at Raft. He was standing, shading his eyes as though staring at the smell. The dawn was at his back, and across the dawn a flight of wild duck was making in from the sea.

Imagine a person walking in a garret from absolute penury to find himself a millionaire. Such a person, were he normal, would feel what the girl felt as the message of that noxious odour struck home to her mind.

Her teeth chattered a little as she rose to her feet. She could not speak and she had to hold her lower jaw with her hand to still it. Then the muscles of her throat did all sorts of queer things on their own account and a violent feeling of sickness seized her that would have ended in an attack of vomiting had it not passed as quickly as it came. Raft, who had ceased staring to the west, saw how she was taken and put his hand on her shoulder.

"You'll be all right in a bit," said he, "it comes hard at first. I've seen chaps go clean off their heads sniffin' land after three months of hell and weather. We'll start in a bit, there's no call to hurry, and I'll just take a walk to get the stiffness out of my legs."

Off he went, away and away, disappearing beyond a dip in the ground.

She knew that he would be away at least half an hour. Thoughtful as a mother for her comfort, yet almost as outspoken, sometimes, as a nurse, he was wonderful.

The dawn broke broader and stronger, peaceful and grey, promising a continuance of the fine weather that had now lasted for three days, three days without wind or rain or threat from the mountains that sat this morning far away and clear cut against the sky.

Then as they went on their way the sun broke over the edge of the high lands and gulls rising above the cliff edge flitted like birds born of snow and fire.

They stopped for ten minutes to breakfast, then they went on, and now suddenly came something new. On the wind they could hear the sound of gulls quarrelling, a sound quite distinct from the ordinary mewing and wheezing of the gulls at peace.

"We're near there," said Raft. "Hark at the gulls, they're fighting over the scraps. Them chaps, whoever they are, have been killing seals and boiling the blubber. The bay's there."

He pointed to a higher rise in the ground just before them and to the fact that the land from there sloped down inland at a terrific rate.

He was right.

Ten minutes walking brought them to the end of their journey and to the edge of a cliff two hundred feet high. It was as though a giant had taken a gouge and cut a bay right through the sea cliffs. Far across the water of the bay before them the land rose again in a precipice steep as the one on whose edge they stood.

The ripples of the bay washed in on a beach of black pebbles easily reached by the declivity of the land and on the beach, stewing like witches' cauldrons, queer looking try-pots were sending up their smoke. Near the pots carcases of sea-bulls lay ripped and gory and being cleared of their blubber by small men, strange-looking, stripped to the waist and with arms and chests splashed by blood.

But the clove in this devil's mixture was the ship moored in the cliff shadows, a small ship like a withered kernel in the shell of the bay, barque-rigged, antiquated, high pooped, almost with the lines of a junk. One might have fancied her designer to have taken for his model some old picture of the ships of Drake.

The try-pots, carcases and busy men left Raft unmoved. The ship held his whole mind.

"Lord! Look at her," said he.

XXXI

The Ship

S he had been built on the Chu Kiang in the great Junk building yards that lie just below Canton and her bones had been put together by yellow men. Built to a European design China had come out in her lines just as the curve of the Tartar tent tops still lingers in the roof of the pagoda.

She might have been a hundred and fifty tons, not more, maybe less, and the junk pattern had been eliminated and European sticks and decent canvas substituted for lateen sails by the direction of the man who ordered her and who was a smuggler.

She had been built for swiftness as well as cargo and, her builders having been junk builders since the time of Tiberius, she was a failure, sailing like a dough dish; and the yard that built her, having seen her float off, went on building junks.

Then she passed from hand to hand, and dirty hands they were, from the Chu Kiang to the Hoang Ho, and through the Korea Channel into the Japan sea, trading sometimes, smuggling sometimes, and once, as far as the Kuriles, sealing in forbidden waters. She was caught by the Russians and her crew clubbed to death or sent to the quicksilver mines and then she came back to China, somehow, by way of Vladivostok and was sold and sold again till she fell into the hands of one, Chang, a sea scraper to whom everything came in handy from bêche de mer to barratry and murder.

Chang was modern in some of his ideas, he carried a Swenfoyn-harpoon gun and, having luck down by the Sundas, he collected half a cargo of oil which he sold at Perth; from Perth he had dough-dished along down to Kerguelen after the "big seals." He had struck this bay by chance and he had struck oil, for all to westward of it lay a stretch of unwashed rock, as good a sea elephant ground as that on the long beach.

The girl standing beside Raft viewed the scene below her with a catch at the heart. The carcases, the little blood-stained busy men, the try-pots like witches' cauldrons and that strange-looking ship which even to her eyes seemed not as other ships were, all these had a tinge of nightmare. Amongst the men she noted one, big almost as Raft. He seemed their leader.

"Chinks," said Raft, "Chinee—they've got their pigtails rolled up, well, they're better than nothing."

He picked up the bundle that he had laid down and led the way to the slope that gave on the beach.

As they came on to the upper part of the beach the "Chinks" noticed them, paused for a second in their labours and then, finding that it was only a solitary man and woman, went on with their work as though the intruders had been a couple of penguins.

"Cool lot," said Raft.

The girl paused. The sight of the carcases and the blood at close quarters, the absolute indifference of the blubber strippers at the sight of an obvious pair of castaways, the whole scene and circumstance turned her soul and chilled her heart.

"I don't like this," said she. "Those men make me afraid, they don't seem human—they are *horrible*."

"Wait you here," said Raft.

He advanced alone across the black shingle and she stood watching him and listening to the stones crunching beneath his feet.

His advance did not disturb the workers.

They seemed working against time. Without any manner of doubt they were anxious to be done with the business and be out of that bay before the next blow came, for the place was fully exposed to the west-nor'west and a storm out of there might easily break their ship from its moorings and send her broadside on to the shingle.

Undersized, agile, with weary-old faces that seemed covered with drawn parchment, they seemed less like men than automata; all save the leader, a gigantic, imperious-looking Mongolian with a thin cat-like moustache, a man of the true river pirate type with a dash of the Mandarin. This man held in his hand a long thong of leather. Captain or leader, or whatever he might be, he was most evidently the serang of that labour party.

On the shingle where the ripples washed in lay a boat, half-beached.

The big man was Chang, and as Raft approached harpoon in hand, she saw Chang draw himself up to his full height and stand waiting. Then she heard Raft's voice and saw him pointing at her and inland and then at the ship.

Chang stood dumb. Then all at once he exploded, shouting and gesticulating. She could not make out what he said, but she knew. He was ordering them off. He seemed to be ordering them off the earth as well as the beach. And Raft stood there patient and dumb like a chidden child.

Then she saw Raft nod his head and turn away.

He came back crunching up the shingle. "Sit down," said he.

She sat down and he took his seat beside her. He had dropped the bundle just there, and as he sat for a moment before speaking he noticed that the fish line securing the mouth of the sack was loose, he carefully retied it.

"You saw how that chap carried on," said he, "I had to put a stopper on myself. He's the chap; them little yellow bellies don't count. He's the chap, and I've got to get him aside from the others." He spoke rapidly and she saw that his eyes were injected with blood.

A new fear seized upon her, a fear akin to the dread she had felt that dark night in the cave when she had caught the sound of La Touche dragging himself close to her, the dread of imminently impending action.

"Let us go away," said she, "another ship may come; anything is better than having a fight with those men."

"Have you got that knife safe?" asked Raft. She still wore the fisherman's knife round her waist. She put her hand on it.

"Yes, the knife is safe."

"If that chap downs me for good," said Raft, "stick that knife through yourself. If he doesn't you take my orders and take them sharp."

He had risen to his feet and without a word more he came down the shingle again towards the workers, walking in a leisurely way and trailing the harpoon along.

He approached Chang who turned on him again with the anger of a busy man importuned by a beggar. The most heart-sickening thing to the girl was the way in which, after the first driving off of Raft, the great Chinaman and his crew had gone on with their work as though they were alone on the beach. Pity and humanity seemed as remote from that crowd as from the carcases they were handling. Active hostility would have been less horrible, somehow, than this absolute indifference to the condition of others.

Chang did not wait for Raft to speak, this time; he began the speaking, or, rather, the shouting, advancing on the other who began to retreat. Chang, as if wishing to have done with this matter for good, followed him up and at every step the devil in him seemed to rise higher whilst his voice filled the beach.

What a voice that was! Half-singing, half-booming, the "whant-whong-goom-along" of the running coolie chanting as he runs seemed mixed with it, till, his anger breaking bounds, he let fly with the strap in his hand, catching the other across the shoulder of the arm that held the harpoon.

Then Raft killed him.

The girl who saw the killing was less appalled for the moment by the deed than the doer of it. The blow of the harpoon that sent Chang's brains flying like the contents of a smashed custard apple was like a flash of lightning, it was the thunder that terrified.

Roaring like a sea bull he sprang from the body of Chang towards the crowd who faced him for a moment with their flensing knives like a herd of jackals. The girl, who had sprung to her feet, plucked the knife from her belt and came running, terror gone and a wind seeming to carry her over the shingle; zoned in steel blue light she saw the harpoon flying from right to left destroying everything in its way, knives flying into the air as if tossed by jugglers, a yellow greasy back into which she struck with her knife, a yellow Chinese face falling backwards with eyes wide on her, as if the Chinese soul of the creature she had stabbed to the heart were trying to cling to her.

Then she was sitting on the shingle very ill and Raft was coming back to her, running.

The fight was over and the beasts had flown, left and right, she could see them crawling like ants away up on the higher ground. They had dropped their knives and the knives were lying here and there on the shingle where also lay four dead bodies including the body of Chang.

Ten minutes ago there had been fifteen live Chinamen on that beach.

Raft was bleeding from a cut on the arm, his face was gashed above the beard, a knife had ripped his coat and the back of his left hand shewed another wound.

He was laughing and carrying on like a man in drink and now that her stomach was relieved an extraordinary light-headedness seized her. Like Raft, she seemed drunk.

She had been snatched for a moment into a world where to kill was the only alternative to death or worse than death. For a moment she had lived in the Stone Age, she had fought like a savage animal and with the fury of the female, more terrific than the rage of the male. She had been pushed to the edge of things, and it was she who had turned the fight. The man she had killed was in the act of knifing Raft in the back.

"The boat!" cried Raft.

She struggled to her feet, steadied herself, and came to the boat. They pushed it out till it was nearly water borne; she scrambled in, he followed, and pushed off. Out in the bay the high black cliffs rose above them as if pushed by a scene shifter, the light-headed laughing raving feeling left her, and as they came alongside of the barque to starboard and tied up to the channel plates she was clear headed and calm and able to get on board by the channel without assistance.

On the deck she tottered and fell in the dead swoon of exhaustion.

It is a long journey to the Stone Age and back and the man or woman who makes it is never quite, quite the same again.

HENRY DE VERE STACPOOLE

XXXII

The Opium Smokers

Raft had never seen a female swoon before. He thought for a moment that she had dropped dead and the shock of the business pulled him together like a douche of cold water. Then he saw that she was breathing and took heart, rubbing her hands and poking her in the ribs and calling on her to pull herself together. He would have been more frightened only that he put her condition down to her general unaccountableness in some ways.

In less than five minutes she had come to and was leaning on her elbow and declaring herself to be all right. Then she got on her feet and, taking her seat on the side of the open hatch, looked about her at the dingy deck cumbered with a whale boat and all sorts of raffle. The slight swell of the bay rocked the barque to the creaking tune of block and cordage, whilst overhead the sea-gulls flitted mewing against the vast black cliff that rose three hundred feet sheer from the licking sea.

"You're all right now?" said Raft dubiously.

"Yes, I feel quite right and strong again—just a little dizzy, that's all."

"Mind and don't tumble back down that hatch," said he, "I'll drop below and see what's to be found if you keep your eye out for them Larrikens. Give me a call if you sight them."

The Larrikens were nowhere to be seen; they were in the high ground hidden, and no doubt holding a council of war, but sight or sound of them there was none.

She nodded and he dropped below into the cabin.

The cabin of Chang was clean, almost dainty. Two smaller cabins opened from it, one evidently for Chang and the other for his second in command. Raft in his hurried look round saw a lot of things including a rack containing six rifles and two heavy revolvers resting on an ammunition box filled with hundreds of cartridges. He opened the lazarette beneath the cabin flooring; it seemed well-stored, and on a shelf in the main cabin there were some provisions including a tin of biscuits.

He brought up the biscuits, the two revolvers and a pocketful of ammunition and, taking his seat on the hatch edge beside the girl, opened the tin; then he went forward and hunted for water, found the water cask and, getting a tin pannikin from the galley, brought her a drink.

He had never loaded or fired a revolver; the girl had, and she shewed him how, the echoes of the cliffs answering to the ear splitting reports as he made a few practice shots, and the guillemots squalling and rising in clouds from their perches on the rock.

"We're fixed all right now," said he, "and we can have those chaps on board when they're ready to come."

"On board!"

"Oh, they'll come right enough, they've got no grub on land."

"Come—but do you mean to say you will let them?"

"Who's to work the hooker out of the bay?" he answered, "Not you and me. We've got to get them aboard. There's no harm in them now they're licked."

He spoke with a knowledge of men absorbed from the whole world over. The Chinese were licked and like dogs they would come to heel. He knew it, for he knew men. He had put the fear of God into them, he and the girl; the thing was over. Give the "Chinks" time to lick their wounds and swallow their gruel and they would be right as pie. He had seen a whole ship's company licked by a little man of great will, and in hundreds of experiences and fights he had found that a beaten man, be he strong as ten, is to be led like a child. He was right. Next morning—they slept on deck that night keeping watch alternately—the "Chinks," hungry and starving for a suck at their opium pipes appeared, the whole eleven of them, and coming down the beach like a troop of children stood in a line; then they began to wail.

Wail and wag their heads and wave their hands. Kerguelen, coming on top of the licking, had broken them to pieces. Then the whole lot kow-towed like one man, knees and forehead on the shingle.

Raft got into the boat and rowed off for the beach bringing them aboard four at a time and as each lot reached the deck they kow-towed to the girl and then trotted forward to the fo'c'sle, disappearing like rats, their teeth chattering from exposure during the night, stripped to the waist as they were, and never could one have imagined these little cringing harmless looking men the jackals of the day before.

When the whole lot were in the fo'c'sle Raft gave them time to settle, then he went down amongst them revolver in pocket. They had lit a lamp, some had lit opium pipes and some were lighting them, and they lay about like creatures broken with cold and weariness. He nodded to them and left them to the opium that would drive the chill from their bones, then coming on deck stood beside the girl.

"They'll be able to work the ship tomorrow," said he, "told you they'd be all right; reckon they won't mind changing that big chap I knocked out for us."

"They don't seem to be able to speak a word of English," said she.

"Oh, I reckon I'll do the steering till we get clear of this place," said he, "they'll handle the sails without knowing English and once we're clear we have only to make north till we strike a Christian ship."

"They seem so harmless," she said, "and when I think of that fight— and of what I did—"

"You fought fine—damned fine," said Raft, "damned fine." He put his arm round her, not as a man puts his arm round a woman, but as a shipmate puts his arm round a shipmate.

XXXIII

Mainsail Haul

That night Raft and the girl took it in turns again to keep watch on deck. They might just as well have gone below for all the trouble the crew could have given them. These gentry had fought bitterly because they had been attacked. Raft had frightened them. There is a form of bravery which one might liken to inverted terror. Rats shew it when they are cornered, and so do men. They had seen their boss killed with a blow and the destroyer hurling himself on them and, though they were peaceable men, they fought. These same peaceable men, be it understood, would, all the same, have murdered a human being for profit could they have done so with reasonable safety.

When the girl came on deck in the morning, after her watch below, she found the deck busy and Raft with his hands in his pockets leaning against the port bulwarks and watching the busy ones.

"They're in a thundering hurry to get out," said Raft. "That chap," pointing to a "chink" that seemed a cut above the others and was evidently the mate, "has been pointing to the sky and out there beyond the bay. They seem to smell bad weather coming. I nodded my head to him and he's working the hands now for all they're worth."

"The wind is blowing from the land," said the girl.

"Yes," said Raft, "it'll take us out without towing, unless it changes."

The hatch cover had been put on and the boat brought to the davits, some of the crew were up aloft scrambling about like monkeys, others were making ready to haul on the halyards and a fellow was unlashing the wheel. There was not a face in all the crowd that did not bear the signature of Anxiety writ on parchment.

The fear of weather, the fear of Kerguelen, and the fear of that bay, which was evidently haunted by evil spirits, drove them like a whip.

The mainsail was set to a chorus like the crying of sea fowl and the foresail and jib. The tide coming in held the barque to a taut anchor chain with her stern to the beach and the wind ready to take her. The mate was at the wheel and now from forward ought to have come the sound of the windlass pawls and the rasp of the rising anchor chain. It

HENRY DE VERE STACPOOLE

didn't. From the group of Chinese collected there came, instead, a clang followed by a splash.

"Why, the beggars have knocked the shackle off the chain," cried Raft. "Lord bless *my* soul, never waited to raise the mud hook?"

"Does it matter?" she asked.

"Sure to have a spare one," answered he, "but it gets me, that's Chinee all over, they're rattled."

"Look!" she cried, "we're moving!"

The cliff's were beginning to glide landward and the bay's mouth to widen, sea-gulls flew with them screaming a challenge, and the guillemots lining the cliff ledges broke into voice, echoes and guillemots storming at them as they went.

Then the sea opened wide under the grey breezy day and the great islands shewed themselves away to the east. To the west and the north all was clear water.

Raft and the girl walked to the after-rail and looked at the coast they were leaving; it seemed horribly near and the great black cliffs only a gunshot away. If the infernal wind of Kerguelen were to arise and blow from the north even now they might be seized and dashed back on those rocks, but the south-east wind held steady and the cliffs drew away and the coast lengthened and new cliffs and bays disclosed themselves, till they almost fancied they could see, away to the east, the great seal beach where the remains of the dead man lay in the cave and where the great sea-bulls were without doubt taking their ease on the rocks.

And now came the last call of Kerguelen, the voice of the kittiwakes:

"Get-away—get-away—get-away."

Raft, as they stood and watched, put his arm over the shoulder of the girl and as she held the great hand that had saved her and brought her so far towards safety her mind, miles away, kept travelling the long road from the caves.

"I'm thinking of the bundle and all the poor things in it," said she, "it will lie there forever on the beach, waiting to be picked up—it's strange."

"I was thinkin' the same thing myself," said Raft, "and the old harpoon I licked that chap across the head with."

XXXIV

The Carcassonne

Raft had found other things than arms and ammunition in the cabin, he had found a box containing nearly three thousand five hundred dollars, partly in American money and partly in English gold coin. Chang had stowed it in his chest, a big cedar-wood affair containing all sorts of oddments, including a can of blue label Canton opium, cigars, a couple of suits of fine silk and a woman's gold bracelet.

Chang had evidently been well-to-do in his way and a man of refinement. His bunk bedding was of the finest quality and on a shelf near the bunk lay piled new-washed sheets and pillow cases. The girl took his cabin and slept in his bunk. Long ago, in the world that was slowly coming back to her, the idea of sleeping in the bunk of a Chinaman she had seen killed would have revolted her, now, it did not trouble her at all. She only knew that a mattress and clean sheets were heaven, even if she had to sleep with a revolver under her pillow. Then in a day or two she only put the revolver there as a matter of routine. The "Chinks" gave evidence that so far from making trouble they were extremely anxious to propitiate and please, and the man who had evidently served Chang appeared in the cabin tidying things and laying out the food, whilst the man who had evidently been mate worked the ship in his own weird way seeming scarcely ever to sleep. He had laid the course almost due north, taking the sun with a back-stick that might have come out of the Ark, working out his calculations in the fo'c'sle in his own head. Raft did not know, he knew nothing of navigation as a science, nor did he care, they were going north and day by day drawing into the track of ships, that was enough for him.

One day the girl said to him: "Suppose these men make trouble over that man you killed—and those others."

"Let them," said Raft, "I'll tell my yarn—it's plain enough—I'm not going to tell no lies. The chap tried to drive us off, and we lost and near done for, and he hit me a welt on top of all. He got his gruel."

She had played with the idea of making up a story for the sake of Raft; she felt ashamed of the idea when she heard his words.

"I'm thinking of that money down below," said he, "it belonged by rights to that big chap. If a ship takes us off we'd better hand it over to the mate or just leave it there for him to take."

"Yes, we don't want the money," she replied, "I have plenty."

"You! Where have you got it?" asked he, looking her over.

"In France," she replied. Then she laughed. It was the first time she had laughed since that day when the sea-bulls had driven the penguins off, and Raft, as though her mirth were infectious, laughed also.

It seemed a joke to him, somehow, the idea of her having money in France.

The idea of her being one of the Rich People had never worked its way into his head. She was just herself, different it is true in some indefinable way from anyone he had ever met, speaking differently, acting differently, but made used to his mind by struggle and adversity. He scarcely thought of her as a woman, yet he was hugely fond of her, a fondness that had begun in pity and had been strengthened and made to grow by her pluck. He liked to have her near him and when she was out of sight he felt a bit astray. He never bothered about the future, so the idea of parting with her had not come to him.

And she? When Raft was out of her sight she felt astray. Her mind had spun between them a tie, of a new sort in a world grown cynical and old and cold; an affection permanent as the hills, warm as summer. Everything good in her loved Raft, it was the affection of a mother for a child, of a child for a mother.

He had nursed her back to life, he had brought her life, and never once since that day had he chilled her with a littleness or broken a thread of what was spinning in her heart. He was illiterate, he was rough, but he was Raft. He was the great beach of Kerguelen and the sea-bulls and the distant islands, he was the hand that had destroyed Loneliness and driven away Death, the child who had listened to Jack and the Bean Stalk, the Lion that had destroyed Chang, the companion in a loneliness ringed with despair.

One morning beyond the 40th parallel, and some two hundred miles to the nor'west of St. Paul, the Chinese mate plucked Raft by the sleeve and pointed into the west.

The day was clear with a wind just enough to fill the sails of the barque and a long blue leisurely swell running from the south. Away in the east was a trace of smoke as though a grimy finger had stained the sky just above the sea-line.

"Ship," said the mate.

It was the one word of English that he knew. Raft was about to shout and run to the cabin hatch to call the girl. Then he held himself back. It might be a false hope. Yet if he had thought he might have known that a ship in the east meant a ship right across their course, here, where there were no trade tracks north and south.

Then above the sea-line and clear of smoke he saw her hull.

He pointed to the halyards and the mate understood. The mate was evidently desperately anxious to be quit for good of his self-invited passengers, for when Raft came on deck again with the girl they found the barque under bare poles rolling to the swell and a Chinese flag half-masted flicking in the wind.

Also, away across the sea, sheering towards them and making to cross their bows a mile away a two funnelled steamer whose funnels closed to one as she shifted her helm to get within speaking distance of them.

She was the *Carcassonne*, a seven thousand ton freighter carrying passengers, a French boat, bound from Sydney to Cape Town and Marseilles.

Raft, the day before, had taken the Chinese mate down to the cabin and shewed him Chang's money and had presented it to him and the crew in pantomime.

It was honesty. It was also a good stroke. There was no trouble when the *Carcassonne*, her huge bulk rolling gently to the swell, dropped a boat, though indeed had the companions of Chang wished to raise trouble they would have found themselves seriously handicapped, dumb as they were in every language but their own.

Chang had been their linguist as well as their leader. They had literally lost their tongue.

HENRY DE VERE STACPOOLE

PART VI

XXXV

MARSEILLES

On board the *Carcassonne* the girl had broken down as though all the exhaustion she had defied had waited for that moment to fall upon her.

But the energy that had held her above defeat and had given her hope when things seemed hopeless was there, undestroyed, and when the turning point came she rallied swiftly. She came on deck one morning where Bathurst lay a point invisible beyond the blue sea to starboard and sitting in a deck chair made friends with the other passengers.

It seemed to her almost impossible that the same world should hold Kerguelen and at the same time this paradise of azure blue sky and tepid wind.

Raft had told her story before reaching Cape Town and the loss of the *Gaston de Paris* was now old news in Europe, and the fact that of all the *Gaston's* crowd only the beautiful Cléo de Bromsart had been saved.

Raft had joined the crew of the *Carcassonne*, sleeping in the foc's'le, where there were several English speaking sailors, and as much out of his element as a man used only to masts and spars can be on a steamboat. However, he swabbed decks and did odd jobs without a grumble and he was swabbing the deck on the morning she came up; he dropped the business for a moment to take the two hands she held out to him.

All through that time below she had been wanting Raft and his big hand to pull her through. Satisfied, knowing he was on board and all right, but wanting him all the same.

On the old barque once or twice had come the stray thought of how Raft's figure would accommodate itself against the background of the world she knew.

Well, here was the world she knew, or part of it; a deck, clean as a ball-room floor and as spacious, passengers in deck chairs, reading novels, and a manicured French surgeon ready to talk art or philosophy to her, polished, but rather narrow of shoulder.

And against all that stood Raft, rough and in the clothes he had worn on the beach, for there was not a man on board whose clothes would have fitted him comfortably.

Well, he was not incongruous with this background, simply because he destroyed it. In a ball-room it would have been the same. He carried with him his background of high black cliffs and miles of beach and flying gulls and breaking sea, and in a flash came to her the fact that he dwarfed and belittled the other people around just as nature dwarfs and belittles art.

She held both his hands for a moment, managing to pat them, somehow, as she held them, asking him what on earth he was doing with the swab he had just dropped. She had an idea that the ship people had put him to work, but before the idea had risen to indignation heat he reassured her.

"I must be doing," said Raft. "Not that there's much to be at in this old kettle. You've got your legs back, well, that's good. I had it out with that doctor chap and he told me how you were going from day today, but I've been wanting the sight of you."

He put his hand on her shoulder as he might on a pal's, then he crossed his arms. "And well you look," said he.

"Doctor Petit," said the girl, speaking in French, "this is Raft, the bravest and best man in the world as you will know when I tell you all. Shake hands with him."

The doctor shook hands.

The passengers, and the first officer, across the bridge canvas, watched all this with curiosity. They knew something but they did not know all. They did that night when she had told them as best she could.

After that she met him often on deck, giving him a word or stopping for a chat, and it was now that she began to think and make plans as to the future.

Raft had become part of herself, they were bound together as perhaps no two such contrary beings had ever been bound. The idea of Love, the idea of Marriage, all conventional ideas as between grown-ups of opposite sex were as absurd in relation to them as they would have been in relation to two children who had grown attached one to the other.

As regarded one another they were in fact two children, for Raft had never been anything but a child and Kerguelen and Raft combined had awakened the primitive and the child in her, giving her the power of affection that makes a little child throw its arm round the neck of a dog.

But the world could not understand that, and Raft to the world was a rough sailor man, and she, to the world, was Cléo de Bromsart.

She would lie awake at night listening to the pounding of the screws and thinking of this—contrasting the figure of Raft with the world she knew and the world she knew with the figure of Raft.

Madame de Brie, her nearest relation, would pass before her mind's eye with her gold eye glasses, and the Comtesse de Mirandole and a host of others; and the queer thing was that the vaguest feeling of antagonism tinged her mind towards these estimable people. They seemed forgeries, impudent forgeries of the handwriting that had first written the word Man on the earth. She had seen the original writing.

She felt also towards them the antagonism of the child to the grown up, and of the person who can't explain to the person who stands waiting for an explanation.

Then she would laugh quietly to herself, for no woman, surely, was ever in a similar position. Then, casting her mind back, she would sometimes choke a little with tears in her throat, tears for herself, dying of loneliness, and for the hand that had brought her back from death.

They passed the entrance of the straits and Gibraltar, and one bright blue winter's morning they entered the harbour of Marseilles, with Marseilles before them blazing in the sun and the bugles of Fort St. Jean answering the crying of the gulls and the drums of Fort St. Nicholas.

Cléo was dressed in the same clothes she had worn on her escape from the *Gaston de Paris*. She had borrowed a hat from one of the ladies on board and stockings and other things from another lady; but she still wore round her waist the leather belt with the empty knife sheath.

As she stood on deck, now, waiting whilst the *Carcassonne* berthed at the wharf alongside a great Messagerie steamer, she carried over her arm the oilskin coat and, by its elastic band, the sou'wester. They were old friends.

Then when the hawsers had been passed and the gang plank was being run out she saw amongst the crowd on the wharf Monsieur de Brie and Madame de Brie, also a number of well-dressed people, Parisians some of them.

Then she was being embraced by Madame de Brie and trying at the same time to acknowledge the salute of Monsieur Bonvalot, her lawyer and man of affairs, a stout pale man with long Dundreary whiskers who had come from Paris to receive her.

All this crowd had not come purely on account of Cléo. Beside the people interested in her there were several friends and relations of Prince Selm, also his lawyer.

"I have taken rooms at the Hotel Noailles," said Madame de Brie, "and I have brought you some clothes. Oh, my poor child, what you must have suffered. But why did the people on board not lend you some better things?"

"Oh, my clothes are all right," said Cléo, "people wanted to lend me things, but I am quite comfortable in these."

She was looking about in search of Raft who was nowhere to be seen.

Then she was seized by the rest, by the Comtesse de Mirandole, by Madame de Florey, and several others who had stopped at Marseilles— on their way to Monte Carlo—to meet the *Carcassonne* and greet the girl who had alone survived the wreck of the *Gaston de Paris*, some of these people knew her only slightly, but once a person becomes famous or notorious it is astonishing how slight acquaintanceship blossoms into full friendship.

Several photographers from the illustrated papers were amongst the crowd and a Pathé operator was on the quay.

Cléo was already recovering that sixth sense, which one might call the social sense, and, as she talked almost to half a dozen people at once, answering questions and receiving felicitations, this sixth sense told her quite plainly that she was being criticised by her felicitators, that in their eyes she was a guy. That the old velour hat she had borrowed, the hair that shewed beneath it, her face, which had still upon it a reflection of Kerguelen, her old skirt and coat—all these things, singly and taken together, were exciting in the minds of these Parisians a pity which was not unrelated to humour. She did not mind, she was looking for Raft.

It seemed to her that all these people, excellent in their way, had a tinge of unreality about them. On the voyage she had sometimes vaguely dreaded that Raft might be pushed away from her, despite herself, by the contrast between him and her own order. It had come to her that the difference between the beach of Kerguelen and the Avenue Malakoff might take her like a giant of mind and divorce her from her allegiance to him. That the good companion, the true friend, the person she loved might alter completely under the touch of social alchemy.

Raft was impossible. She knew that. More impossible even than a sea elephant from that far beach where life was real and Paris a dream. Impossible in Paris where life was false and the far beach a dream.

Raft at a dinner party! Raft at one of those elegant afternoons where the talk would run on the politics of the moment, on symbolism, on

Bergson, or Iturrino or the works of Othon Friesz—! He could not be her companion in that place, in that atmosphere, within leagues of those people.

She was not thinking that now. "These people" around her seemed strangers; they had in fact always been strangers, strangers who had kissed her, conversed with her, dined with her, but strangers; the one, true, living, warm friend, the only one she had ever known, was Raft. It was the penguins and sea-bulls over again, the polite, bowing, absolutely correct penguins, the warm lumping, living sea-bulls.

Her heart, chilled by stephanotis-scented kisses, words of felicitation and the fat smiles of men in tall hats and tight-buttoned overcoats, chilled by Monsieur de Brie's gold rimmed eye glasses, chilled by a social state that had never warmed her, cried out for Raft. Kerguelen and that beach, where, even now, the sea-bulls might be lingering, seemed a warm and blissful vision, real, alive, a place where life meant living.

Ah, here he came. He had been helping to fix a hawser at the bows. She ran towards him.

"Ah, there you are. Now, you are coming with me. I have told the captain and he said this morning it would be all right as you were not signed on."

"Right," said Raft, "but where are you going?"

"To an hotel."

He looked about him. He saw the crowd on deck but he did not connect it with her. He was out of his reckoning. He had never thought of what would happen in port as regarded her, or where he would go or what he would do; making plans was not in his way. In the ordinary course of things he would have gone to the British consulate and the Shipwrecked Mariners' people would have returned him, carriage paid, to England. He had always been in the hands of others and of chance.

She—he had always called her She, and here, be it said, he did not know her name, never having asked—She had now taken him into her hands and he felt vaguely that she was a power on this new beach where he was stranded.

Had you told him that she was a woman of society and very wealthy his idea of her power would not have been increased; he knew nothing of wealth or society. She was She in her old dress that he knew so well, and still carrying the sou'wester he had fetched from the cave where she had done that chap in, and as for any idea of being under an obligation to her for food or housing he had none. He would have done the same for her.

Yet, to tell the truth, the docks, with no money in his pocket and the cold prospect of brilliant Marseilles, had made him feel adrift like a lost child. Civilisation had affected him as it had affected her, so that something, now, made him put his hand on her shoulder to get the touch of her, and she, knowing that every eye in all that party behind her was upon them, took the great hand and held it and patted it.

It was as well to take her stand at once, though she was scarcely bothering about that. Then, still holding his hand, she came along that white deck towards the gang-plank. The officers knew and, as they bade her goodbye, they nodded to Raft, but the Parisians knew nothing but that Cléo had gone clearly mad—and that that awful sailor had placed his hand on her shoulder, familiarly!

There were several automobiles waiting by the wharf and Madame de Brie, half-dumb and slightly agitated, having pointed out the car she had reserved for Cléo, the girl introduced Raft.

"This is Raft who saved my life," said Cléo.

Then she took Raft by the arm and pushed him into the seat beside the chauffeur; having done that, she got into the car, following Madame de Brie. The Comtesse de Mirandole got in, also, followed by Monsieur de Brie and his gold eye glasses.

The mistral was blowing so that the windows of the car had to be kept closed.

Used to fresh air, the girl nearly choked at first with the stuffiness of the car. The olfactory nerve is really a prolongation of the brain, as though the brain, distrusting the other senses, had pushed out a trustworthy scout to see what the world and its contents were really like. The sense of smell never lies; it is of all senses the truest and it handed along without comment to the brain of Cléo the faint perfume of the stephanotis affected by Madame de Brie and of the Yoya-yoya affected by the Comtesse de Mirandole, also traces from the varnish and upholstery of the car.

"Who, my dear, is that man," asked Madame de Brie. She had almost said "that dreadful man" but she had checked herself.

"Man—Oh, that is Raft. He saved my life."

"How delightful," said the Countess, "and he seems quite a character."

"Quite," said Madame de Brie half-heartedly, "but my dear Cléo, you will excuse an old woman for suggesting it, your generosity must be

HENRY DE VERE STACPOOLE

on its guard, he placed his hand on your shoulder, quite familiarly it seemed to me."

"Well," said the choking Cléo, "why should he not? I have slept with my head on his chest on a rock and I have stabbed a man who was trying to kill him. Between us we fought a whole crowd of Chinamen. He had a harpoon and I had a knife and we beat them and took their ship. Do you mind having the window a wee bit open? I feel rather faint."

"That's better," said she to the speechless other ones, "I'm so used to fresh air that I can't bear to be closed in."

"But my dear Cléo," suddenly broke out the old lady, "what do you intend to do with him?"

"Do with him? Nothing. He's my friend, that's all. Ah, here we are."

The car had drawn up in the courtyard of the Hotel.

XXXVI

The Leper

Déjeuner had been prepared for the party in a private room, a big room, for there were twelve guests all told, including not only Cléo's friends but the business men, and the friends of Prince Selm.

But before thinking of déjeuner or anything else she had to see about Raft.

She left him standing in the hall whilst she interviewed the manager.

Actually, the business would have been easier for her had she brought with her an animal, even of the largest pattern. The manager, when he had caught a glimpse of the intended guest, revolted; not openly, it is true, but with genuflexions and outstretching of hands.

Where could this man be put, what could be done with him? The valets and ladies' maids would certainly not eat with him, the visitors would object to his presence in the lounge, the servants in the servants' quarters. He was a common sailor man. Heavens! What a problem that manager had to face, something quite new, quite illogical, yet quite logical. He had heard of the wreck of the *Gaston* and he was as interested in Cléo as a hotel manager could be. He understood the whole case when she told him that Raft had saved her life; he was a man of broad mind, but he knew intimately the mental make up of his servants, his visitors and their servants. He discussed the matter with Cléo quite openly and she saw the reason of all he said. Raft was "impossible" in that hotel. His heroism did not count a bit; it did with the manager who would not have to sit at table with him, it did not with the waiters and valets and ladies' maids who would have to associate with him, or the guests whose eyes would be offended by his presence.

"He belongs to a ship," said the manager. Then he solved the question with a burst.

"I will look after him myself." He ran into the hall and called Raft to come with him; then, followed by Cléo, he led the way to a sitting-room, a most elegant sitting-room upholstered in blue silk.

"Here," said he to the sea lion, "will you take your seat and déjeuner will be served to you."

"I have to leave you for a bit," said Cléo, putting her hand on his arm, "I won't be long."

"I'll wait for you," said Raft. He was a bit amazed at all the new things around him and blissfully unconscious of trouble. He threw his cap on a chair and took his pipe from his pocket, the same old pipe he had lit that night on the ledge of the sea-corridor, then he produced a plug of tobacco, the same tobacco whose pungent fume had comforted her there, with the sound of the hungry sea coming through the dark.

Then he sat down on a silk covered chair and the manager and the girl went out.

"I will serve him myself," said the manager. "I understand; he is a brave man but very rough; the servants do not understand these things. It is a difficulty, but after—? Mademoiselle—after?"

"After what?"

"After he has had his meal?"

She understood. After he had been fed he was to go. He could go, say, to a sailors' lodging house; she had heard of such things. Or, he would walk about the streets; the thing was quite simple. It was only right to give him a good meal and some money, a good round sum, seeing all he had done for her.

She was scarcely heeding the manager. She was viewing, full face, the truth that the manager had demonstrated to her clearly. Raft was impossible. She had had vague ideas of bringing him to Paris and giving him a room for himself in her house on the Avenue Malakoff. She had never thought of the servants, she had thought of her friends and that they would think her conduct queer. But she saw everything now quite straight and in a dry light. Raft was shipwrecked on a social state; to keep company with him she would have to renounce everything and live on his level; she could not treat him as a servant; even if she could, servants would resent him. He was not of their type, much lower, a labouring man from the sea. Not to lose him as he was to her she would have to enter the absolutely impossible and absurd, she would have to give up social life and make a world of her own with Raft. With a man whose setting was the sea, the wilderness, whose life was action, who was ignorant of art, philosophy, the convenances, who was a figure of scorn to every educated eye when caught against the background of Civilisation.

In three beats of a pendulum all this passed through her mind.

Then she said to the manager:

"Quite so. I understand. I must thank you very much for your real kindness. I shall give this man a sum of money, and this afternoon you will be free of him. He can find shelter at a sailors' home—I have heard of such places."

"Oh, Mon Dieu! Yes," said the manager, vastly relieved, "and either I or Fritz, my head waiter, will serve him with his food. Fritz is a man of temperament and knowledge and I will explain to him."

He hurried off and she was left alone in the corridor.

She opened the door of the little sitting-room. The leper was seated hunched on his chair just as she had seen him sitting often on a rock; he was surrounded with a cloud of tobacco smoke.

She had seen the loneliness of Kerguelen but that was nothing to this.

Poor Raft. The very chairs and tables shouted at him; he looked ridiculous. How in her wildest dreams could she have entertained the idea of holding him to her, here?

He would have looked more ridiculous only that he looked, what he felt, forlorn. The place was beginning to tell on him, used to the rough and the open; the smooth and the closed were getting at him.

When he saw her he took the pipe from his mouth and pressed the burning tobacco down with his finger nervously, the same finger she had sucked once when parched with thirst.

She saw, as a matter of fact, that he was nervous, if the term could apply to such a huge and powerful organism, and the fear came to her that if left alone he might bolt before she could conduct him in person to the Sailors' Home.

Standing with the door held half open she nodded to him.

"I want you to stay here," said she, "till I come back. I have to talk to all those people you saw and I may be a couple of hours. That man will bring you something to eat—you don't mind my leaving you here?"

"Oh, I don't mind," said Raft "but you'll be wanting something to eat yourself."

"I'll get it."

"You'll come back, sure?"

"Sure."

She laughed, nodded to him, and closed the door. Her cheeks were flushed and her eyes bright, she was strangely worked up; a touch might have sent her into a storm of anger or a burst of tears.

HENRY DE VERE STACPOOLE

In the corridor she met Madame de Brie who had been hunting for her.

"Cléo, they are waiting déjeuner for you—but, my dear child, you have not changed, has no one shewn you to your room?"

The old lady had not only brought along Cléo's maid who, with the rest of the servants, had been on board wages during her mistress's absence, but a trunk full of clothes.

"I am not going to change," said Cléo, "I am too busy—and too hungry—"

A reporter from the *Gaulois* stopped her as she was turning towards the room, indicated by Madame de Brie, where déjeuner was to be served.

"Mademoiselle," said the reporter, "I did not like to trouble you sooner, may I crave the honour of a short interview with you on account of the *Gaulois*?"

"Certainly, monsieur," replied the girl. "Pray come to déjeuner as my guest, I hope to tell my friends something of my experiences and what I say you can repeat; that will be better than a formal interview tête-à-téte, which, after all, is rather a depressing affair."

The déjeuner was not a depressing affair. Cléo struck the note. She was in radiant good humour. Madame de Brie sat on her right, Monsieur de Brie on her left. Monsieur Bonvalot, her man of affairs, with his long Dundreary whiskers, opposite to her; the rest were scattered on either side of the long table.

At first the conversation was general, then, after a while, Cléo was talking and the rest listening.

"As I shall be very busy for a long time," said Cléo, "I would like now to give all the information I can about the loss of the yacht. A gentleman is present on behalf of the *Gaulois*, and as all details I can give relative to the disaster are of world wide interest, considering the position of the late Prince Selm, I take this opportunity of making them known. Unfortunately they are few."

She told briefly but clearly the story of the disaster, of her escape and landing on Kerguelen, of the caves and the cache and the death of the two men. She did not tell how La Touche met his end, that business had to do with no one but herself and La Touche. She gave it to be understood that he, like Bompard, had met his fate in the quicksands.

She told of her loneliness, and how she had been dying simply from loneliness, how she had been saved by Raft and how he had nursed her like a mother.

It was then that she really began to talk and shew them pictures. They saw the beach and that terrible journey along under the cliffs, cliffs that seemed cut out of night and never ending, the sea, like an obsession, crawling shoreward, and Raft carrying her on his shoulder.

They saw the summit where she had stood looking towards the west and the hopeless prospect of finding a bay that might not be there and an anchorage where there might be a ship, on a coast where few ships ever came.

Fascinated and warmed by Perrier Jouet, they followed her to the place where the wind had brought her the smell of the try pots and to the cliff edge where Derision shew her the Chinese whaler and the terrible little man, blood-stained, and busy with butchery.

She shewed them the great serang—Captain of the Chinese—driving them off the beach and telling them to begone back into the wilderness, and, vaguely, the fight where Raft had saved her from death or worse—

"Ah, Mon Dieu, what a man," cried a female voice down the table.

Cléo stopped.

"Yes, Madame la Comtesse," said she, "but a man beyond the pale, a man to be ashamed of, a man who, were he to sit in the lounge of this hotel and smoke his pipe, would drive all the other guests away. A common sailor. A man rough from the sea and illiterate."

There was a dead silence.

Monsieur Bonvalot, a socialist, though a business man, nodded his head. He broke the silence.

"A man," said Monsieur Bonvalot, "is, after all, a man."

"Oh, no, monsieur, he is not," said Cléo, "not in Marseilles. But do not think I am quarrelling with social conditions. There must, I believe, always be hewers of wood and drawers of water. I am just talking of Raft and my own position as regards him. I am not thinking of the fact that he saved my life time and again, or that he nursed me with his great rough hands as tenderly as a mother. I am thinking of the fact that I have discovered something quite new and genuine, a human heart that is warm and real and true and simple, simple as the heart of a child, a mind that has no crookedness, a man who, in Paris or here in Marseilles, is absurd, not because he is rough and uncouth, but because he is like Monsieur Gulliver amongst the little people. I have seen the great, I have seen the wind and the sun and the sea and the mountains as they really are, and life as it really is, for those who really live. I have seen death, none of you here have ever seen or imagined death, none of you here have ever seen life, none of you here have seen the world. You all have been protected from the truth of things, and fortunately, for the truth of things would break you as it would have broken me but for Raft, who sits in a room at the end of that corridor and whom the manager of this hotel is serving with food with his own hands because the hotel servants would consider it an insult were they asked to carry him his food.

"I am not grumbling. I quite recognise the logic of the whole thing, but I feel as though I were looking at everything through the large end of a pair of opera glasses, just as when as a child I used to do so and amuse myself by watching human beings reduced to the size of dolls.

"Well, now you have all my story and I have put before you a new view of things and I hope I have not shocked you all. My poor Raft must now go to the Sailors' Home where I am going with him. I want some money, Monsieur Bonvalot."

"Mademoiselle," said Bonvalot, awaking like a person from hypnotism and delighted to find himself on a business footing again, "certainly, I have here your cheque book which I have brought with me."

"Then we will go to another room and discuss business matters," said the girl rising. "Now all you people please enjoy yourselves. You are my guests whilst you stay in this hotel. Madame de Brie will see that you have everything."

She led the way from the room, Monsieur Bonvalot following. A suite had been engaged for her and here in the sitting-room she started to talk business with her man of affairs.

A large fortune is like a delicate animal, always in need of nursing and attention, it is always changing colour in spots from rosy to dark, a depreciation in Peruvian bonds means that your capital has shrunk just there and the question comes will it go on shrinking; a big rise in P.L.M. shares suggests taking the profit and re-investing should they fall again.

Monsieur Bonvalot had problems of this sort to set before the girl—she swept them away. "I have no time to attend to all that now," said she, "someother day will do. I want twenty thousand francs, have you got them?"

"Twenty thousand francs," said Bonvalot. "No, Mademoiselle. I brought five thousand francs in notes thinking you would want them for your expenses here, but you can write a cheque on the Crédit Lyonnais and I will get it cashed for you at once."

He produced from a wallet a bundle of pink and blue bank notes and counted out five thousand francs, then she wrote a cheque for fifteen thousand payable to him. He endorsed it, went off and returned in ten minutes with the money. She put the notes in a big envelope and the envelope in her pocket. That same pocket still contained the old tobacco box of Captain Slocum and the other odds and ends which she treasured more than gold.

"That will do for the present," said she, "tomorrow I will open an account at the Marseilles branch of the Crédit Lyonnais, or rather you can do it for me today. Give them this specimen of my signature and they can telegraph to the Paris branch. I would like two hundred thousand francs put to my credit here.

"But are you not coming back to Paris?" asked Bonvalot.

"No, Monsieur Bonvalot, not at present!" He pulled his whiskers.

The idea had suddenly come to him, and come to him strongly, that she was about to do "something foolish."

He had seen women do very foolish things in the course of his business life and all that talk of hers at the luncheon table came back to him now.

He remembered the beautiful Mademoiselle de Lacy who had run off and married a groom; could it be possible that Cléo contemplated any such mad act with that terrific sailor man? The idea chilled his heart.

Equality and Fraternity were parts of his motto and he was an honest socialist; he believed honestly that all men were equals and that the waiters who served him at table were as good as himself, with a difference of course due to the accidents of life, but he believed, with Daudet, that there is no greater abyss than class difference.

His theory was confounded by this practice. But he could say nothing, for the matter was too delicate to be touched upon.

XXXVII

A New Home

Raft was still in the room where she had left him. As they passed through the hall where a number of people were seated about in basket chairs she felt every eye fixed upon her and her companion. Then out in the sunlit Cannabier Prolongué she drew a deep breath just as a person draws a deep breath after a dive.

She also felt free.

She had always been free in theory; possessed of her own money she could have done absolutely as she liked, in theory. In practice she had always been a slave. The slave of a thousand and one things and circumstances, things and circumstances many of them troublesome, many of them wearisome, all of them not to be denied.

"Mademoiselle, your bath is ready."

"Mademoiselle, the first gong has sounded."

"What dress will Mademoiselle wear this afternoon?"

Oh, the day, the day with its hundred phases and divisions, the dresses that went with each phase, the lukewarm emotions and interests and boredom and suppressed hatreds, this thing called the day, which she had first reviewed in the open boat after the wreck of the *Gaston de Paris* terrified to find it torn from her—this thing had been returned to her that morning in all its futility. It seemed to her, as she cast it away, a horrible gaud, a thing made of tinsel, yet a thing that could destroy the soul and blind the eyes and numb the heart.

She had never been free, she had always been the veriest slave, the slave of things, of people, of convenances, and of circumstances.

Doctor Epinard had spoken something of the truth.

Man may not be an automaton worked by environment, all the same he is the slave of environment, and never such a slave as when his environment is that of high Civilisation.

For there the pure motives of the mind have ever to be regulated and falsified, the heart crushed, the face veiled.

To break with all that falsity means shipwreck.

"Which way does the sea lie?" asked the girl. Raft turned to the left as though the smell of the sea were leading him.

"I'm glad to be out of there," said he, "I was near smothered in that place."

"So was I," said she, "did that man bring you your food all right?"

"Another chap brought it," said Raft, "a Dutchman."

She laughed.

"Do you know what I was thinking?" said she.

"I was thinking of the time you brought me food when I was nearly dying. You didn't tell a Dutchman to bring it. I'd have brought you your food myself and we would have had it together only I had to talk to those people. Well, I've got rid of them. How would you like to live always in a place like that hotel?"

Raft mentally reviewed the room done in blue silk, Fritz, and the rest of it.

"I'd rather be out in the open," said Raft. "Not that I have anything to say against it—but I'd rather be out in the open."

They walked along.

Companionship with Raft had for her one delightful thing about it, it was companionship without restraint. In a way it was like companionship with a dog, or a child. Like two old sailors they would hang silent, sometimes, for a long time, not bothering to speak, content with being together.

She had never imagined the possibility of a man and a woman of absolutely different social position in such a relationship, never drawn the ghost of such an idea from all the books she had read, all the plays she had seen. Never could she have imagined a common sailor man striking Art for her to pieces, as he had struck the story of Anatole France, and creating above a world he had taught her to despise, a nest for her mind rough as himself, but in air pure and living.

Raft, the common man, had made her social world seem vulgar as well as small, chill as well as vulgar.

She was thinking just now as she walked beside him how when she had told him that the hotel manager would bring him something to eat, he had said, "but you will want something to eat yourself." That was the sort of thing constantly recurring in all sorts of ways that had brought her to know him truly, occurring in little ways as well as in that great and heroic moment when he had told her to destroy herself with the knife if he were killed.

As they passed along the Cannabier they saw a drunken sailor reeling along towards them through the crowd, and Raft drew her by the arm off the sidewalk to avoid him.

The sight in other times would have made him laugh, or more likely it would have been scarcely noticed, but She, in some manner or another, made drink discreditable, and the sight of it to be avoided. It would have been the same, most likely, had he been taking a child for a walk. Down near the docks they passed a birdshop before which Raft cast anchor almost forgetful of his companion. There were all sorts of birds here, those tiny birds from the African coast one sees in the shops of the Riviera, canaries and parrots.

There was one parrot, enormous and coloured like a tropical sunset, drowsy-eyed and insolent looking. When he saw the sailor man he seemed to rouse up. He looked at Raft and Raft at him.

"I'd like that chap," said Raft, "he beats the lot of them."

"And you shall have him," said she.

He laughed.

"Much good he'd be to a chap like me. Where'd I keep him?"

Her eyes softened as she looked at the bird and from the bird to the man. Where, indeed, could he keep him? He who had no home—nothing. Then it was that Money seemed to her what it really is, a god, beautiful and benign.

It had often seemed to her as a demon, but Raft, who unconsciously had cast ridicule on her world, was now, unconsciously, shewing her the great truth she had never seen before, the truth that Money is more beautiful than Apollo, more etherial than Psyche, more powerful than Jove.

"You will soon have somewhere to keep him," said she, "we will get him tomorrow. Come on. I want now to find the place where the fishing boats put in. I saw it the last time I was here in Marseilles, years ago, but I am not sure of the direction."

She asked a man who was passing and he pointed the way; it was a long distance, but it seemed short, so full was her mind with the plan she had formulated before leaving the hotel. She talked as she went. Talked just as though they were on the Kerguelen beach hunting for a cave.

"We will find a place to put the parrot. I want a great big boat, not a yacht. I've had enough of those. I want a good sea boat and the fisher-boats I have seen here seemed to me good, and the men are the right sort of men. I am going to buy one—or hire one—well, we shall see. I want you to help to get it ready for us. How good the smell of this place is," she paused to sniff the tar-sea scents brought by the afternoon wind. It was like the smell of Freedom.

Then they came on to the fisher wharf and right into the arms of Captain Jean Bontemps.

Captain Jean was about five feet in height and he seemed five feet in thickness. He was propped against a bollard and he was in his shore-going clothes. The girl's eye told her at once that here was a useful man, a man of authority and knowledge. She approached him, and as he took his pipe from his mouth and removed his cap, she opened her business without parley or hesitation.

She wanted to buy or hire a fishing boat, price no object.

He did not understand her at first. He seemed suffering from some form of deafness. Then when she repeated the statement he shewed no surprise.

He himself was a fishing boat owner, Captain Bontemps of the *Arlesienne*, and he was quite willing to sell his boat, for a sum—two thousand pounds he asked, and she did not know that he was speaking in jest, just as one might speak to a child.

"If your boat suits me, I will pay what you ask," said she, "let me see it."

Then it came upon Captain Jean that he was either talking to a lunatic or some wealthy woman with a craze. His sails were taken aback and he was left wallowing in a heavy ground sea of the mind with a smell of spice islands tinging the air.

La Belle Arlesienne, his old boat, was not worth a thousand pounds. Under the hammer heaven knows what she would have fetched, but she was his wife, or the only female thing that stood in that relationship to him. He tapped the dottle out of his pipe, then he took a pouch from his pocket and began to refill and the girl, seeing his condition, drew him aside, asking Raft to wait for her.

They went to another bollard and there, the mariner anchoring himself, she began to talk. She introduced herself. He knew all about the *Gaston de Paris* and Mademoiselle de Bromsart. He put his pipe in his pocket, finding himself in such famous company. She went on. In ten minutes she told him her whole story, told him just what Raft was and just how they stood related, and just how he had been treated in the hotel.

"It's as though they had turned out my father or my brother," said she, "we two who have fought and faced everything together have grown into companions. Friends who cannot be parted, Captain Bontemps. If he were a woman or I a man it would be easier. As it is things are difficult. Well, I do not care. I will do exactly as I like. I feel you will be my friend, too; you understand me. And I want you to look after him tonight, for in the whole of Marseilles I do not know where he could go unless to some wretched Sailors' Home or worse. Ah, it is wicked. Of what use is it to be brave, to be honest, to be true in this world?"

"Mon Dieu," said the Captain, "I will look after him, if for no other reason than that he is what you say, mademoiselle; but *La Belle Arlesienne* is rough, should you use her as a yacht, you would not find her a yacht. She smells of fish—"

"I am used to rough things," said the girl. "I dread the smooth. Captain Bontemps, for one who has done for me everything should I dread anything? And a little roughness, what is that to freedom and the life I have learned to love with the man I love? For I love Raft, Captain Bontemps, just as I know he loves me. Oh, do not mistake me, it is not the sort of thing they call love here amongst houses and streets, it is not a woman that is speaking to you but a human being."

He understood her. To his broad and simple mind the thing was simple; she did not want to part with the man who had saved her and fought for her and who had been "chucked out" of a hotel because he was a rough sailor, and marvellously well he understood that when she said she loved Raft she did not mean the thing that the dock side called Love. No Paris poet could have understood her. The old fisher captain did.

But he was a practical man. He struck himself a blow on the head.

"I have what you want," said he, "*La Belle Arlesienne*, no, it is no use, I have something better, a good cruising boat—you say money is no object."

"None."

"Then come with me, you two."

He led the way followed by Raft and the girl to a wharf where a tug lay moored and by the tug a fifty ton yawl.

"There's your boat," said Bontemps, "built by Pinoli of Genoa for an American. She has even a bath-room—a main cabin with two cabins off it, your man could berth in the fo'c'sle which is big enough for twenty like him. Follow me."

He led the way on to the deck of the yawl.

The girl went over it down below into the main cabin with two little sleeping cabins off it. She peeped into the tiny bath-room, examined the pantry well-stored with crockeryware, there was everything even to the bunk bedding, sheets and towels, she went to the fo'c'sle; compared with the fo'c'sle of the *Albatross* it was a little palace.

Then she turned to Raft.

"This is your new home," said she, "there is room for your parrot here." Then turning to Captain Bontemps. "Well, that is settled and now I only want a crew and a captain—fishermen. I will have no yachtsmen on my boat. I have had to do with yachtsmen, Captain Bontemps."

"Oh, my faith," said the old fellow, "you will easily find a crew."

"Yes, but I won't easily find a captain. I want you."

The Captain laughed.

"And how about *La Belle Arlesienne*?" asked he.

"You must leave her behind you to be sold. In my service money is no object. Now as to this boat, who is the agent from whom I can buy her?"

"Latour and Company," replied the old fellow, for the first time in his life in the powerful grip of wealth and not knowing exactly whether the great golden hand was holding him heels or head up.

"How far is Latour's from here?"

"Not far."

The girl stood for a moment looking round her at the white deck, the masts, the rigging, and as she looked some hand seemed to draw aside a veil revealing the stupid immovable houses of the land filled with stupid immovable people bound and tied up by soul-killing conventions—and on the other hand the old mystery of ships, those homes of Freedom on the road that has no boundaries.

Then she turned to Bontemps.

"Come," said she, "let us go to Latour's."

"CLÉO," SAID THE DISTRACTED MADAME de Brie, writing to a friend, "Cléo must always have been as mad as her aunt De Warens. Fishermen, it seems, are the only honest people, and she and her cargo of fishermen, with an old man named Bontemps, are now heaven knows where since I met them at Portofino.

"She calls them her children and when I last saw her she was coming along the little quay at Portofino helping that big red bearded man to carry provisions.

"The times are revolutionary, that's the truth, and women are not what they were, and I am old, I suppose, and cannot see things as I ought to see them—and the grief is she might have married anyone, she might have married Royalty itself, and I told her so and she laughed in my face. She said she never intended to marry anyone, that she already had a family of 'children' and that the great bearded man Raft was the smallest of them all, that she was teaching him to read and write and to talk French so that he could converse with the rest of her family.

"She has made Portofino her headquarters, it seems, and she is the lady bountiful of the fishing folk there, sits in their cottages and talks to them, taking up her quarters at the little *auberge* and sometimes living on board her boat.

"A strange life, and yet she seems happy, like that poor Mademoiselle La Fontaine, whom I last saw at the Maison de Santé of Doctor Schwanthaller, seated with a straw crown on her head and imagining herself a queen."

There ended the letter of Madame de Brie, and here ends the story of Cléo de Bromsart, a woman of energy and mind who learned from Kerguelen that Life is an endless striving, not a peaceful drifting, and that of all things high the highest is the soul of a child.

THE END

A Note About the Author

Henry De Vere Stacpoole (1863–1951) was an Irish novelist. Born in Kingstown, Ireland—now Dún Laoghaire—Stacpoole served as a ship's doctor in the South Pacific Ocean as a young man. His experiences on the other side of the world would inspire much of his literary work, including his revered romance novel *The Blue Lagoon* (1908). Stacpoole wrote dozens of novels throughout his career, many of which have served as source material for feature length films. He lived in rural Essex before settling on the Isle of Wight in the 1920s, where he spent the remainder of his life.

A Note from the Publisher

bookfinity & MINT EDITIONS

Enjoy more of your favorite classics with Bookfinity,
a new search and discovery experience for readers.
With Bookfinity, you can discover more vintage
literature for your collection, find your Reader Type,
track books you've read or want to read,
and add reviews to your favorite books.
Visit www.bookfinity.com, and click on
Take the Quiz to get started.

Don't forget to follow us
@bookfinityofficial and @mint_editions

CPSIA information can be obtained
at www.ICGtesting.com
Printed in the USA
BVHW041226260122
627130BV00021B/2135